Whale Fall

ELIZABETH O'CONNOR

Whale Fall

PANTHEON BOOKS, NEW YORK

All rights reserved. Published in the United States by Pantheon Books, a division of Penguin Random House LLC, New York, and distributed in Canada by Penguin Random House Canada Limited, Toronto. Originally published in hardcover in Great Britain by Picador, an imprint of Pan Macmillan, a division of Macmillan Publishers International Limited, London.

Pantheon Books and colophon are registered trademarks of Penguin Random House LLC.

Library of Congress Cataloging-in-Publication Data
Names: O'Connor, Elizabeth, [date] author.
Title: Whale fall / Elizabeth O'Connor.
Description: New York : Pantheon Books, 2024.
Identifiers: LCCN 2023029366 (print) | LCCN 2023029367 (ebook) | ISBN 9780593700914 (hardcover) | ISBN 9780593700921 (ebook)
Subjects: LCGFT: Novels.
Classification: LCC PR6115.C667 W47 2024 (print) | LCC PR6115.C667 (ebook) | DDC 823/.92—dc23/eng/20230830
LC record available at https://lccn.loc.gov/2023029366
LC ebook record available at https://lccn.loc.gov/2023029367

www.pantheonbooks.com

Jacket images: *North Wales* (detail) by Frederick William Hayes.
Photograph © Nottingham City Museums & Galleries / Bridgeman Images; (woman) Malivan Iuliia / Shutterstock
Jacket design by Kelly Winton

Printed in the United States of America
First American Edition

2   4   6   8   9   7   5   3   1

I have looked long at this land,
Trying to understand
My place in it.

R. S. Thomas, 'Those Others'

Whale Fall

Here is an island year. First the sun, and first the spring growing fat with birds. They leave the island to its grey winter and return when shoots appear in the ground. Auks come as dark shapes under the water. Kittiwakes and gannets fall from the skies. We do not notice them at first. The children might chase them on the cliffs, the men fishing might push them away from a net with an oar. By the end of spring they are thrown across the island like shadows. Puffins, sea swallows, little terns. By summer they are raising young, flinging themselves back into the water.

The kittiwakes come closest to our houses, picking food scraps from the middens in the yard. They perch on the roofs: from afar the building is spiked with the grey points of their wings. They live on the roof, covering it in a silver layer of feathers and guano, waking us inside as they squabble and scurry across the tiles. Sometimes they fight mid-air, leaving red smears on each other. They drop fish from their beaks onto the stone yard, which worm into the stone's small crevices and holes and make them smell rancid for months. The heat only brings them closer: their bird-smells, their calling, their pink-dead young.

In summer, the women of the island repaint the houses white. They go into the limestone cave at the west of the island and chip the rock into powder. My mother would always return with it on her hands, specks trailing everything she touched. Sometimes the pigment turned the paint more yellow, or more blue, than pure white. One year the houses all over ended up a pale rose-pink and it still shows through, in nicks and patches where the outer layers are peeled away.

After summer, the cold circles, then drops like a stone. The birds disappear one by one. They leave their nests on the cliffs with eggs still inside. In autumn, the sea boils like a pot on the fire. The birds pass and the summer is gone.

Winter: we stay near the hearth, sleep in the same bed. The sea sidles up to the door, laps at the edge of the island. There is grey ice at the horizon. The wind makes red meat of us. At Christmas we cook a catch of fish, then butcher a sheep, and throw it into the water. The waves push it back onto the beach again by spring, and the birds arrive to devour it. The sheep are rotated around the island, after they've grazed their field to nothing.

September

The whale became stranded in the shallows of the island overnight, appearing from the water like a cat slinking under a door. No one noticed it: not the lighthouse with its halo of light on the water, or the night fishermen searching for whiting and sole, or the farmers moving cattle over the hill at dawn. The sheep on the cliffs were undisturbed. Under the dark water, the whale's body glowed lightly green.

By the morning it had floated up onto the beach, and lay neatly on its front. Birds gathered above it. The tide brought water over the sand in wide, flat mirrors broken by thin paths of sand. The waves drew around the whale and then out again, like a membrane around its delicate centre.

Some of the fishermen said it had come off course. They saw them out at sea but rarely so close. A few older people said it was some kind of omen, though could not agree on whether it was good or bad. Reverend Jones read the English newspapers most weeks but he said there was nothing that could explain the creature's arrival. The navy was newly out at sea since the start of the month. He made a vague suggestion about radar and one of the farmers nodded and said, *submarines*.

Someone brought a large camera down from their house, a box which sat on long wooden legs. The flash made the landscape bleed out.

I was born on the island on 20th January 1920. My birth certificate read 30th January 1920, because my father could not get to the registration office on the mainland before then. There was a great winter storm and no one could leave the island. When we were finally able to cross, my mother used to tell me, the beach was covered in jellyfish, like a silver path of ice. My mother survived the birth, thank Jesus, because no one could have come to help her.

The island was three miles long and one mile wide, with a lighthouse marking the eastern point and a dark cave marking the west. There were twelve families, the minister, and Polish Lukasz who worked in the lighthouse. Our house, Rose Cottage, was set into the side of a hill, where the wind wrapped a fist around it. Tad said the army should have made tanks out of our windows, the way they stood against the weather. The glass had warped and splintered in places but still held fast to the frame. In the bedroom, at night, you could hear our neighbours' goats calling out to their young through a crack in the pane, and sometimes you could see a candle in their house burning like a coin balanced on the top of the hill.

~

Tad always called me by the dog's name. On the day of the whale, he passed me in the yard, calling for the dog. I was trying to clear dust from the hearth-rug, but watched as it formed a silvery layer over my clothes instead. I had to bat the midges away from my eyes.

'I'm going on the boats, Elis,' Tad said.

'Manod,' I said. 'Not Elis. Elis is the dog's name.'

'I know, I know that.'

He waved me away. He headed down the path towards the sea. His rubber boots made a sucking sound on each step.

'That's what I said,' I heard him say. 'Manod. That's what I said.'

On the other side of the yard, Tad dried mackerel by stringing them up on a line. He loved the dog: there was one section of dried fish just for him. My father barely spoke to me or my sister, but at night I heard him mumble long conversations with Elis. In the yard, Elis ran circles sniffing at the lichen between the slabs of stone, barely stopping, barely looking up at me. I cut a fish down for him, and he ran into the hawthorn ungratefully, sending up a small cloud of dried dirt and leaves.

I rubbed at a smear on my dress. It was an old one of my mother's, dark flannel with loose threads trailing at each hem. Mam made her own clothes and then taught me. She made them practically, with wide pockets and space for moving around. I liked to copy the patterns in the magazines women left behind in the chapel. Mainland trends. From them I realised most people on the island dressed ten years behind everywhere else. Sometimes suitcases were washed up the shore and in them I found old garments to wear or take apart for the material. I found a ballgown once, with only a small tear at the hip, in anemone-red silk. It had a small pocket on one side, and out of it came a gold-plated powder compact, shaped like a scallop shell. The powder puff was still orange from contact with its owner's skin.

~

Our neighbour appeared soon after Tad left, his clothes and hair dripping. I could see him come over the hill to where his wife was milking one of their goats. I could smell him from where I stood, the damp of his sheepskin jerkin and his soaked shirt beneath. His wife ran to him and cupped his face. I felt awkward watching them, and stood combing my fingers through my hair. I could hear snatches of what he told Leah: *We thought it was a boat. Do you think it's a bad sign?* I watched Leah's hands stiffen, the breath catch in her throat.

Not one person on the island knew how to swim. The men did not learn how, and so neither did the women. The sea was dangerous and I suppose we had lived with its danger too long. A popular saying amongst them: Out of the boat and into the water. Out of the frying pan into the fire. Out of the boat and God help you.

There used to be a king on the island, who wore a brass crown. When he died in the previous decade, no one wanted to do it anymore. Most of the young men had been killed in the war, or were trying to get a job on the mainland. The ones left were too busy on the fishing boats. So it goes. According to my mother, the women were not asked.

My sister spread butter over bread with her fingers, eating the bread and then licking her fingers one by one. You're too old for that, I told her, and she stuck out her tongue at me. I poured tea into three cups on the table, and watched it steam.

Llinos turned the cup around in front of her, as though inspecting it from every angle. She combed her fingers through her hair. I thought of something my mother used to say about us: *Ni allaf ddweud wrth un chwaer oddi wrth un arall.* I can't tell one sister from the other. There are six years between us, but only one of us is still a child, so that is no longer true.

'What's the English word?' I asked her.

'I don't know.'

'Yes, you do.'

Llinos gulped her tea, and winced.

'Hot,' she said.

'It's whale.'

I looked over to Tad to support me. I had been trying to improve Llinos's English all summer but she was stubborn. Tad sat with his head hanging back, his eyes closed. One hand in his lap and the other holding Elis's muzzle. His clothes were drying in front of the fire, mixing the smell of laundry with the smell of fish. Ours was a small front room: space for a table, chairs, fire and a small dresser. The dresser was covered in drips of candle wax. Tad had taken out his dental plate with its three pearlescent teeth, and left it in the centre.

By the door was a bucket with the lobsters he had caught that day. In the silences of our conversation, I could hear them move in the water, claws scraping against the bucket's metal side. I watched a shadow rise and fall on the other side of the room, and realised it was my hand. I collected the plates and asked Tad if he had seen the whale.

'Out at sea,' he said, rubbing a calloused patch on his knuckles, 'normally you see more than one.'

'Didn't Mam used to talk about whales?' Llinos said.

Dark turn. 'Surely they are bad luck.'

'You sound like a mad old woman,' I said.

I cleared our plates, gave the scraps to Elis on the floor. Tad held my wrist after I took his cup, then moved his hand over mine.

'Marc was asking after you today. Said how nice you looked at chapel.'

'And what did you say?'

Tad shrugged.

'I told him to ask you.'

'You can tell him no, I don't want to.'

Tad sighed and looked at his hands.

'You should be thinking about getting married. It doesn't have to be Marc. It could be Llew.'

'I'm eighteen.'

'The time goes fast.' His voice softened. 'I can't have you here forever.'

'Who would look after Llinos?'

Elis had reared up onto his hind legs next to Llinos's chair, twisting his head to lick up crumbs from the table. Llinos turned and caught his front paws. She stood up next to him, so that they looked like a couple dancing. They swayed from side to side, and Elis opened his mouth wide and panted.

I looked at the bottom of my cup. The milk had formed a film over the surface and puckered, like a strange kiss.

~

In the night I dreamt of a long dinner table, with whales dressed in formal clothes laughing over their plates. I was with them, in a dress I saw in a magazine once, made of pear-green silk, and a hat with a long white feather. Afterwards they danced and I could not say how they were moving, if they were on the tips of their tails or sliding from side to side, just that I was lifted from my feet and spun and spun around. The ceiling was made of lace and velvet, and slowly fell down to me.

I had only been a month away from school. The school was in an old farm building owned by the chapel, large enough for the ten or so children on the island to be taught in its two rooms. We had a desk each, damp wood, and mostly read the Bible. Sister Mary and Sister Gwennan came for a few months at a time, in between teaching at a school on the mainland. The books they brought us had stamps in the front cover reading *Our Lady of the Wayside* in faded gold lettering. We wore white on special days like St Dwynwen's day.

I had a friend at school. Rosslyn sat next to me for ten years and then went to the mainland to marry a quarry worker in Pwllheli, a man with a pink face and an unkind mouth. Rosslyn had met him a few times before she left, visiting his town when her father rowed to the mainland market. At the back of the classroom she confided in me about his meaty breath, the things he said to her. On the day she left the island for good, her father had filled his small boat with flowers and grass. His crying could be heard from the dunes. Rosslyn had curly hair and a round face that shone always with sweat. I always thought she looked like a model I had seen once, on a small card that came with a bar of soap. She sent me a letter after she married; saying she missed me, that she lived in a house with an indoor toilet. The end of her letter asked me what I was doing, and what I planned to do. I had not replied.

I was good at school. Sister Mary called me 'bright' and let me visit her on Saturdays, where she would show me large maps and let me borrow her English novels. When one of the boys applied to a university in England, he asked Sister Mary to check his application, and Sister Mary asked me to do it. I left two spelling mistakes in on purpose, but he still got a place. He said that he would write to me about it, but he never did. His mother showed me a photograph of him on a boat on the river, wearing a long black coat. I had begged to keep the photograph, not because of the boy in it but because his face was slightly washed out, meaning that I could pretend the person in the boat was me.

On the last day of school my teacher had not even said goodbye. She said, *I'll see you at the market.*

The tide was high. Tad's tide calendar, the one he would leave behind for us, did not say that it would be. The calendar was typed out on pink paper, and he was given a new one every season when he visited the mainland. He said he did not need it, judged the tide by sight like his own father had. I did not like to remind him of the times he had been incorrect, when he had come home with damp trousers and shoes filled with sand.

I walked down to the beach to see the whale for myself. When I walked alone I liked to daydream, sometimes about working for a wealthy family on the mainland as a seamstress, or being a nun somewhere in Europe, living in a tall white tower in a city square. In my head I recited Bible verses in an English accent, and made the shape of each word with my tongue.

I followed the people to find the whale. The cove was flat and I could see bodies crowded together. The sand was damp and sucked at my shoes.

In the water, where the rocks were covered in waxy black and yellow seaweed, four men were guiding a bull onto a boat to take it over to the mainland. One walked circles behind it, guiding it forwards. Another stood in the water, next to the centre of the boat, ready to grab it by the horns and hold it still. One waited inside the boat with a coil of rope around his shoulders, ready to attach the bull to an iron ring in the hull. The bull walked slowly, flicking its head. When the man on the beach came closer to it, the bull kicked up its feet. The bull was black, with a thin white stripe down its nose, a bright fissure.

When I passed the men, the one on the beach stopped and turned to face me. He took his hat from his head and did a funny little bow. I ignored him, and the other men laughed. The boat swayed, and the bull ran past them. It ran into the water, and the men cried out. I walked on faster, listening to their shouting, the waves, the bull's snorting.

The water was pale brown, and the froth reminded me of when Tad boiled sheep heads on the stove, fleece around the rim of the pan. I watched it come closer to my feet, only inches away, and retreat back again. I hated when water got into my shoes.

As I got closer to the crowd of people around the whale, I saw that there were birds there too, flying in circles and diving at something. One flew right over my shoulder, carrying something in its beak. A boat had been left on its side in the sand, and a cat slunk out from the hull and hissed at me.

I weaved through the people. The rushing of each wave revealed the body of the whale, gigantic and curled against itself. I thought of the way I would tell my sister about it when she returned from school, committing the sight of it to memory, the dark hull of its spine and the fringe of its mouth, bronze in the low-coming light.

Walking back, I turned and thought I saw my mother standing in the middle of it all. She bent down and touched something. There was fog around her hair and shoulders. Her woollen clothes looked wet. When I looked later the rocks were covered in white lichen, its fronds shaped like minuscule hands.

I was lying on Llew's bed, leafing through his mother's books. She kept them stacked on the floor in a pile as high as her pillow, and I picked the one from the top. A romance novel, with a handsome brigadier painted on the front. The pages inside had at some point become damp and then dried out, and were now shaped in waves. Amber spots covered the sides.

Llew lay next to me, staring at the ceiling. He fiddled with his hands on his chest, picking at his cuticles. Llew was the only other person on the island born in the same year as me. He had handed me a note after chapel one Sunday, three months ago. It said: *Hello. I like your pink dress.* I had written a note back: *It is peach.*

He turned over to face me, looking at the quilt beneath us. He was still fiddling, picking a feather out of the rose-patterned material.

'I heard there is a factory on the mainland looking for workers.'

'That's rather vague.'

He scrunched up his nose, asked me why I always had to be like that. He freed the feather and ran it against the back of my hand. I sighed, put the book back on the pile. I did not care much for Llew. But saying yes to him, kissing him, other things, made me feel slightly less peculiar than

I did. I knew that most girls would ask their mothers what they were supposed to do when they left school, what they were supposed to do with men, but I had no mother to ask. All of my decisions felt like trying to catch a fish that did not exist until I caught it.

'What kind of work is it?' I asked.

'In a herring factory.'

'Will you go?'

'Not without you.'

He kissed me on my lips, and rolled his body over mine. His right arm felt cramped up horribly against my side. He put his left hand under my shirt, up to my breast, and his hand was cold. I looked at the brigadier until we were done.

~

Afterwards, we sat next to the fire, our shadows flickering against the wall. Llew's mother was out at her sister's house down the hill. She would be back soon. I had to go, but neither of us moved.

'You will marry me, Manod, won't you?' he asked. He had asked me this each time I saw him, in varying degrees of urgency, since that spring. I had stopped trying to reason with him that I wouldn't, and settled on simply not answering one way or another. On some days I even considered the idea. I wrapped the lace tablecloth around my face on wash-day, and let it trail down my back.

I watched the fire reflected in the glass of the cabinet on the opposite wall. It was made of dark wood, and had glass inlaid into the doors. Inside was all manner of crockery, most of it broken. Llew would open the door of it for me sometimes, and let me look inside. Some of the pieces were whole, forming butter dishes or small egg cups. He would explain that it was his mother's collection, and that she would collect them along the shoreline from where they were washed up. A whole one was good luck. She started the collection when her husband, Llew's father, died at sea, and she had a lot of new, restless time on her hands.

I felt Llew's hot breath against my ear.

'Do you remember Hywel?' he said. 'He left the island and works in a pen factory. His mother says he worked his way up to floor manager. Makes a good living, she says. I could do the same.'

I would reach inside the cabinet and pick out the pieces one by one. Most of them were white, with differently col-oured floral patterns. I liked the patterns that were green or rust-coloured. Most of them were bright blue. I could imagine myself in a kitchen on the mainland, with whole crockery pieces for my guests. I liked to turn the pieces over in my hand and look at the maker's mark underneath. The pieces came from all over the world. Worcester, France, Japan, Nantucket—

'Nantucket,' I said. 'Where is that?'

'Imagine a life where you're not farming, or fishing, and your hands are completely smooth.'

He held out his hands when he said that, as though showing me an enormous catch.

Lobster season on the island began in September. Boats went out between the tides and looked for flat pieces of wood on the water's surface. Most of the boats were half-rotten and covered over with barnacles, the nets flopping over the sides like tongues. They had women's names, mostly, like the *Anna-Marie*, the *Nesta*, the *Glenys*.

The wood was pulled up as it was attached to a rope, and at the end of the rope would be a cage for luring and trapping the lobster. The pieces of wood were sometimes painted, depending on who had put them there. Outside of lobster season Tad left the cages in front of the house, where they stank sourly, and the netting slowly turned white with salt and soft mould.

When the boats came in, I looked out for Tad's boat and helped unload the lobsters into wide, flat buckets that could be piled on top of each other. I always thought the lobsters were very beautiful, speckled like eggs, each one its own shade of blue. Tad would bind the claws together, his hands covered in scars from where they had caught him, the skin raised in pale welts. He called them *the bastards*, not fondly. *Throw the bastards in there*, or, *Three bastards in that bucket, watch yourself.*

When the men had finished unloading the lobsters, Reverend Jones took his black robes from where he kept them in his boat. He pulled them on while walking back up the beach, over the rough suit he fished in. He spat in his hand and flattened down his hair. His cheeks were covered in a web of angry red veins.

We joined him, and prayed thanks for the catch that had come in. Behind us, the sea reared and crashed. The men stood silently, and very still. I looked at the sand, at my father, out at the mainland, and back again.

Sometimes, instead of dresses, I made small embroideries. I used handkerchiefs as the background and sewed notches on top. That night I made one of the whale. I used peach thread to make the people's faces around it, and gave them little hats in red and green. I didn't give them bodies: too fiddly. I sewed birds above them: grey, black and white. Red and orange for the beaks. At the centre, a large whale. I loved the colour of its skin, so I used blue and grey thread interchangeably, so that the thread shone with the pattern of it, like a feather. I pushed the needle through and felt it make contact with my thimble. I did it again, and again, and again, until the room around me grew dark.

Llinos had always been a strange child. Her favourite activity was to collect bones from wherever she could find them, and slowly assemble them into complete animals. When I asked her how she knew what bone came from which creature, she would shrug, and tell me it was something she just knew. She kept the bones in jars around Rose Cottage. Sometimes I took down a jar of jam and screamed at what was in the jar behind it.

The two of us shared a bed, and sometimes I woke in the night to see Llinos staring at an insect on the wall, or a frond of lichen growing next to the window. The previous summer our father had had to shoot a seabird that had flown into the window at a terrible angle, and Llinos had barely flinched; at the shot, at the dark, sticky patch the body left behind on the ground, at the ghostly white mark of its body on the glass. When I asked what Llinos wanted to do with her life Llinos didn't say she wanted to get married, or finish her schooling, or anything else. She said, *Dw i eisiau dal pysgod, a'u bwyta.* I want to catch fish, and eat them.

Llinos got on with other children, but baffled adults. She played with other children as though she was a dog; all wrestling and biting and spit. Mothers on the island hated her, said she had only half a brain. I was desperate for her to learn English, if only to prove something to those women, though I didn't know exactly what.

~

Llinos wanted to spend Saturday finding birds' eggs at the top of the cliffs. I held her calves down as she wriggled on her stomach to the cliff-edge, and reached down to the nests along the top crags. She passed one egg back to me, then two, and I dropped them into her basket. Llinos had a ritual she performed before going egg-collecting, making egg shapes with her foot in the dirt outside our front door. She had done it twice that morning.

At the top of the cliffs, the ground was matted with sea thrift. There were rabbit burrows everywhere, and brown and black rabbits. The black rabbits were descended from one Lukasz had brought back from a mainland market. Some of them had yellow eyes. We had to crawl on our knees so that we wouldn't twist our ankles in the burrows.

I found flowers I could press in my Bible at home. Sea aster, samphire.

'It's something ladies on the mainland do,' I said, to no one. 'I read that in a magazine.'

I placed a yellow poppy into the pages, and squeezed it shut.

'You should speak English,' I said to Llinos. 'You should practise it.'

'*Nid oes ei angen arnaf,*' Llinos replied. I don't need it.

'You will if we leave the island.'

She turned and held my gaze.

'I don't understand you,' she said. It was not worth arguing.

She picked up an empty eggshell, and held it in her palm. She brought it up to my face.

'What did that?' I asked.

'*Neidr. Rwyf wedi eu gweld yn ei wneud.*' Snake. I've seen them do it.

She dropped the egg and stamped on it with her foot.

When we arrived home Llew's mother was at our table, her eyes red from crying. I felt a sudden panic. I wondered if I'd left an indentation in her bed, if we'd remembered to straighten the sheets. There were two cups on the table, and a plate with a bread crust in the centre.

'Llew is leaving,' Tad said, by way of explanation, when we passed the threshold.

Llew's mother cried out, pressing her handkerchief into her mouth. She was a thin woman, and when she sobbed the vertebrae of her spine stood out beneath her jumper like thorns. I went over to her, placed my hand on her shoulder. Her hair was coiled in a long plait that reached down to her waist.

'Sorry,' she said, between sobs. 'Sorry. You can understand.'

'You must be proud of him,' Tad told her. 'For the best. He'll find good work, a good wife.'

'A wife?' I said. To my own surprise, my voice came out steady.

Llew's mother nodded.

'He does so want a wife.'

'And with a wife comes children,' Tad said. 'And they'll do better on the mainland.'

I said nothing. He was right.

'That's true. That's true. Thank you.'

She grabbed my father's hand, and squeezed it until it turned white.

They brought buckets of water, soaked blankets and coats and threw them over the whale in an attempt to revive it. The men made a plan to guide it back into the sea, and hauled it into the shallows by the late afternoon. The whale's body drifted out to sea, occasionally rolled lifelessly onto its back. A number of children lay on the beach very still, pretending to be the whale. They dragged each other into the water, screaming, and then back out again.

Men and women gathered outside the chapel. Someone had brought a newspaper, put it up against a wall for others to read. Something happening in another country. Violent nights. Another war? someone asked. God forbid, replied another. We had heard this kind of talk since spring: prices on the mainland steadily creeping up, invasion, arms. Snatches of news soon replaced by some other worry, an infection passing through the sheep, a crack in a wall, dogs left roaming in someone else's field. But it felt as though something was circling us, waiting to land against the shore.

Behind the crowd, a group of cows stood watching, moving cud around their mouths. I pulled my woollen coat around me. The wind blew in the smell of rot from the whale. I reached out my hand to stroke one of the cow's noses, but they turned away lazily, as if no one was there.

There were more empty houses on the island than inhabited ones, left behind by families who had gone to the mainland. There were swifts nesting in the roofs, which had buckled inwards. Bats, wasps, moss, mould. Five different kinds of knotweed. I took Llinos into the abandoned houses in the summers to find shade, and sometimes we would find small objects inside: a doll, a tin fork.

The last time we went was July. There were many carvings on the walls inside, writing on the walls, names and rude pictures. In the smallest house, at the end, facing the water, we found a young couple, a girl from the island and a mainland boy. His small boat was on the beach below. He was undressed to the waist, and they were huddled together in the back room. When they saw us, they shrieked and pulled away from each other. We saw that the girl's dress was loosened at the collar, revealing the lace of her slip beneath. They ran, clutching hands. The girl turned and glared at me. We made the mistake of telling Tad about what we had seen, and he asked Reverend Jones about it. He told Tad to dunk us face-first in the tin bath when it was full of water, to wash out the inside of our heads.

And so the days happened, me waiting for something to break. There was a routine to the mornings. I slathered Llinos in ointment to protect her skin from the cold, making her smell of old meat. I watched the way her face shone with a thick layer over it.

We ate soda bread thick with butter and salt. Tad joined us silently. Llinos scooped the butter onto her finger and licked it off. I got her dressed, removed the bones from her pockets with a shudder. I worked my hair into two thin, pale plaits, took the soap from the basin and used it to smooth them down.

Tad kept photographs on the wall in various states of decay: serious women from the last century in black head-scarves, men with thick beards, boys in overalls standing in front of large creatures hung upside down from a winch, glassy eyes hovering at their shoulders. There were photo-graphs of his and Mam's wedding, Mam dark-haired, her white dress fading into her white skin, and Tad thin, as he still was, with buzzed hair from the army. Between those were Saint pictures, not hammered in but allowed to rest wherever the rough walls formed a small ledge. St Peter, St Brendan, one Tad had found between two planks of wood in the boat. The bottom half was dark and embedded with sand. The saint on the front was crying.

There was only one picture of me. It was taken by Merionn on the hill. I was standing in front of a toy carriage made out of wood, with two wooden horses.

There was one photograph of Llinos, also taken by Merionn with the same camera. Elis was in it too. Llinos was the same height as him, so she must have been only two or three years old. She was wearing white, her baptism clothes, and looking at the camera, smiling, her eyes showing up pale and watery. Elis must have been moving his head when the flash went off. Above his shoulders was only a grey blur, sweeping into the gorse bushes behind.

I did not hear from Llew again. No notes, no visits. On the day he left, I feigned menstrual pains. I lay on my bed and looked at the roughly plastered ceiling, which to me looked more and more like curdled milk.

There was a story my mother used to tell us. She saved it for when she, Llinos and I were foraging on the cliffs. Sometimes, when we were up there, we found crabs that had wandered up from the shore. This was the part that I remembered, because they had round sacs of eggs attached to their underside. I would pick them up and turn them over, and through the thin skin I could see the shape of small round things, the skin dancing with sand and salt. Most days I cannot remember what my mother looked like, but I remember the texture and shape of the crab and the eggs as if they are always in my hands.

The story was this. There was a woman who lived on the island before us, a woman with three daughters. When the sea saw the woman walking on the cliffs with her daughters it grew jealous, and sent up a huge wave. The wave swept the daughters away and left the mother there wet and alone. The woman waited for the sea to return her daughters, prayed to it every day. But the sea could only return them as gulls, who would fly up and cry into her ear.

The island did not have a blue sea, it had a grey one. It was close enough to spray the house with water at high tide, and eat away at the paint. It reached up to our bedroom, the window behind the bed. Sometimes when I woke up and was half-asleep it seemed to have crept up to the house like a flood. The grass outside the window seemed to have grown straight out of it like hair on a gigantic body. Sometimes a gull stared back at me, tapping its yellow beak against the glass.

October

The shoreline shifted towards us with the sediment brought in by the waves. In the mornings whole crowds of crabs scuttled in, washes of red and green. In the cliffs, the gorse grew thick with copper heather and white butterflies. The cow parsley curled brown.

I followed Tad and Llinos out onto the tide-flats to gather mussels one morning. We left early. The paths were lined with frost and the sky blank and quiet. Behind us the lobster fishermen called out to one another. Seals barked. The pools on the tide-flats shone pale, a colour Llinos called snake-belly after we once watched a grass snake on the cliffs turn over slowly and die. Dark birds moved from one pool to the next, something wriggling in their red beaks.

A gust of wind pushed my hair across my head, and I had to turn around to free it from my mouth and eyes. That's when I saw the white boat coming in.

~

Boats on the eastern side of the island meant letters, normally, or sailors using the island as a stopover, and that meant cans of syrupy tinned fruit or salted meats that could be passed around. When visitors dropped anchor near the water's edge, some of the boys would go down on their rusted bicycles and collect whatever the boats had and deliver it to the houses. They could be heard from half a mile away, the way the bicycle and the tyres squealed with rust from all the seawater in the air. Since the previous year, I had started intercepting them. I waited at home for the bicycle to appear by the front gate. The boys handed over whatever they had and I pretended to pass them a couple of coins. The boys pretended to shake their heads, then tapped their lips and I kissed them, waved them off. When they were out of sight, I wiped the damp left on my lips with my hand. Sometimes I cleared my throat and spat it all out.

~

By the time Llinos and I reached the beach, Tad had already waded out to where the boat was moored. A thin rope stretched out from it into the water, straining against the boat's rocking, and a man at the front of it was waving and shouting.

Tad helped the man on board step down from the boat into the shallow water. A woman appeared behind him, holding her hat with one hand, and she stepped down in the same way. The man had rolled his trousers up to thick cuffs, his ankles shining blue with cold. He struggled to stay balanced as he waded towards the beach. When he moved, he looked like the spindly flies that sat on the windowpane in summer. Long-limbed, translucent, clumsy. When he reached the beach he collapsed onto his knees, and vomited.

In the house, the pair of them looked strange, like a pair of birds come to roost. Their eyes darted around the room, and the woman perched on the edge of her chair. The man looked closely at the pictures on the wall, shuffling slowly along the length of it. I was not sure what to say to them.

They had invited themselves for tea after they had landed and introduced themselves. Edward, the man, and Joan, the woman. English accents. Tad was taken aback when Joan shook his hand as Edward did. *And why did you come over now? You need to wait to come between tides*, Tad told them. They asked after accommodation and Tad said, *No hotels, but plenty of empty houses.* He left to go back to looking for mussels. Their cases were heavy. I made Llinos carry the woman's hat box.

Llinos moved a small toy along the slate floor of Rose Cottage. She was pretending to do it, in a way she did often when really she was listening. I could see her eyes behind her thick fringe, watching the three of us.

'Would you like milk?' I asked. Joan said yes.

I had never spoken to English people before. Joan had blonde, neatly styled hair that made mine feel greasy on my scalp. Thin eyebrows fawn-coloured. She looked like the women I read about in magazines, who walked on cobbled streets and rode in motorcars. She produced a handkerchief. It was sky blue, cotton, with white embroidery.

'How was your journey?' I asked.

Joan dabbed her brow. Her face was still pale.

'Quite choppy,' she said.

'Sorry.'

I gave her the tin, and a spoon.

'Oh, it's milk *powder*!'

The amusement in her voice made me blush. I was seized with shame. I wanted to kick the tin under the table. I pointed to Leah's goats grazing just outside the window. Their hairy backs were just visible.

'It's that, or goat milk.'

She pushed her cup towards me. I spooned it out and gave it a stir, trying to push the lumps to the bottom. I watched her hands, the pearlescent cuff buttons of her blouse. The material was green and tightly woven, a texture I had never seen before.

'Your blouse is very beautiful,' I said.

'This old thing.' She thanked me for the milk.

'We don't get many visitors. Otherwise I would have something better for you, of course. Cakes. Iced cakes. Buns. Iced buns.'

'Ah, we know,' Edward said. He and Joan exchanged a look.

He joined us at the table, spooning powder into his tea.

'We weren't supposed to come to the island. It was a . . . spontaneous detour.'

'Are you here on holiday?' I asked them. I knew there were seaside resorts nearby. Llinos and I played a game on the cliff sometimes, where we pretended that we could see the Ferris wheel.

'No.' Joan laughed.

'We're from a university in England. Here for a research project. We thought you might be expecting us.'

'Really? Me?'

Edward waved his hands in a circle.

'You as in the island. We arranged the visit with the minister, Jeremiah Jones?'

'It was quite last minute,' Joan interjected.

'Oh. Yes. He hasn't said anything. Or maybe he has. People don't tell me things.'

'Ask them why are they here?' Llinos said in Welsh, without looking up from the floor.

'Llinos, speak English. Don't be rude.'

'That's all right,' Edward said, turning to face her. 'We've been learning Welsh. Spoke it all along the journey. *Beth ddywedoch chi?* What did you say?'

Llinos looked at him and laughed. A high laugh, sharp and mean. I told her to go out into the garden. She left without looking at me, and slammed the door behind her.

'Sorry,' I said. 'She understands. She's just being naughty.'

The silence between us fell awkwardly. I could see Llinos standing at the window behind the couple's heads.

'We heard about the island in Abergele,' Joan said. 'In a pub, one of the fishermen told us about the whale that was washed up here.'

'It's still there.'

Joan nodded.

'Will you go through these photographs with me?' Edward asked, moving back towards the wall.

I told him about each one. My great-uncle, Bryn, who moved to Llandudno and became a butcher. My father's twin brother, Marc. We only had a drawing of him. Someone on the island made it. Emlyn, Marc, my father's uncles. All killed in the war. Llinos, Elis. And my mother, her portraits, her always wearing lipstick. She would go to the mainland every Easter Sunday to get photographs taken in a small studio there. I could have told him what colours the lipsticks were, despite the photographs being black and white, because I had stared at them so long I had them memorised. Red, crimson, orange.

When I turned back towards Joan, she was writing in a small leather-bound notebook. Her brow was furrowed. I panicked.

'Sorry. Sorry, is this boring?' I asked her.

'Not at all,' Joan said, with much certainty. 'I'm writing down everything you say.'

She looked up at me and smiled, colour back in her cheeks.

~

After they left, I could not settle. I cleaned their cups three times. I wished I had asked what the project was. What the university was. More about them both. Edward's accent cut his words down into neat, sharp little chunks, the kind of voice I had only heard on the wireless in Leah's house. I could not remember what they looked like. I asked Llinos, *What did they look like?* and Llinos shrugged.

We sat in two chairs next to each other and waited for Tad to come home. I thought that I should be working on another embroidery, but could not will myself to move.

'The man was handsome, wasn't he?' I said.

Llinos's chest rose and fell against my arm.

'And the woman. The woman was very handsome too. Wasn't she?'

Llinos wriggled and buried her face in my shoulder. She asked me to sing something to make her go to sleep. I sang the first thing I could think of, an old song we sang at school about a black mare someone buys at a fair. The buyer feeds the horse up to make it strong, but ends up making it fat. The mare gets so fat that she dies, and becomes a feast for magpies and crows. Llinos was snoring gently by the final verse, in which the singer asks for money to buy another mare, and the song begins again. I sang it once more, under my breath. Outside the sea hissed like a swarm of insects. I did not hear Tad return home.

On the other side of the island, the whale returned, this time limp, rolled onto its side. The water was filled with jellyfish, their bodies blistering the sand. The whale's stomach was scored with dark lines, like the bark of a tree. Out of the water and onto the sand, the whale's size became overwhelming. The farmer who found it tried to push it into the water, his dog running yelping circles around them both. He could not stand the smell, the feeling of something moving beneath the skin.

The passage is rough and cold; my partner is devilishly seasick. We are met from the boat by a man and his two daughters. The older of the two girls speaks good English, from school and the Bible she tells us later, but the younger girl speaks only island Welsh. Our first impressions of the island are true to our impressions from others; miles of headland with rock and heather, small stone-built houses with slate roofs. The people show their distance from mainland life almost immediately, with many of them wearing clothes from twenty or so years ago, in thick velvet and tweed, with dense woollen shawls wrapped around their necks and chests. In the girls' house we drink tea. The older girl is surprisingly bright and educated. The younger seems afraid of us. The father goes back onto the fishing boats after we arrive.

When we reach the chapel the minister, Rev. Jeremiah Jones, tells us that the population numbers fifteen men including himself, twenty women, and twelve children. Jeremiah serves us a plate of plaice, the skin of which is spotted orange. He says that the spots are considered good luck, and most islanders eat them. The skin is tough and salty, and he smiles as we both swallow it down.

Mam never gave us her hand. She said she did not like the feel of it. That our hands were sticky and plump. She only let us hold her sleeve. Once Llinos tried to hold her hair and Mam slapped her across her face. We never saw her touch Tad, either, though sometimes we would walk in on them pecking at each other like birds. Like all children we were curious about our births. I would ask her, How did you get us? Where did we come from? And she would reply, I asked the sea, and the sea gave you to me. I dreamt in the night that I came to the door and there was a baby outside, cresting the edge of a wave.

Morning, I could not get the fire to light. The logs were damp from the mild evening. I gave up on it and got dressed. I put on a dress and a brown woollen jumper. I decided against the jumper and took it off. The room was ice-cold and my nipples stood up like points. I put a different dress on, made of thick velvet. I stood in front of the mirror. Pinched my cheeks. Put the jumper back on.

Tad kept one eye on me. He said I was behaving funny after the English people arrived, like a cat before a storm. You forgot to light the fire, he said. I stamped down on one of the logs to show him how soft it was, and he said nothing.

I went out and paced between the house and the chapel. I tried to look for glimpses of the English people, something they may have dropped while walking, a view of them in one of the high windows. There were footprints all along the sand, moving from the water, to the path, up to the chapel and back again, over and over each other, looping around. The dune grass was dying, letting its seeds fall into each print's markings.

I stared at the footprints as I walked, and wondered if any belonged to them.

I thought about going to catch Reverend Jones when he came in from the boats, but there would be too many others around, Tad included. I passed Carys, the wife of one of Tad's friends. She greeted me and I waved back. She stopped and said, *English men. They don't come back for you, you know.* Tad must have said something to her. I laughed like a pig and walked quickly away.

On Sunday we changed into our good clothes and walked a mile east to the chapel. There the houses were built closer together, and sloped down to small lean-tos and tables on the beach which served as a market. I watched the men turn their heads to greet Tad, and then smile to greet me. I kept Llinos close to me, my hand over her heart. I was not pretty: most people said I had nice blonde hair, which only made me want to shear it off.

The chapel was low and moss-covered. A line of white gulls queued across the roof, guano thick as grass despite the minister's regular washing of the tiles. Inside it smelt of damp. A large wooden Mary sat in the rafters on the left side, a St John the Baptist on the other with a wooden sheep. There was a time when the figures were painted in bright colours.

The pews were small and could only fit four or so people. Families sat together. When Mam was alive, our pew was the family pew, and I still thought of it that way. The prayer cushion she used was always next to me, with its tree and sky turned brown with use. Many of the prayer cushions had trees on them. Trees were scarce on the island, because of the wind.

Tad spoke to Leah's husband, who sat on the pew behind us. Dafydd had a wireless and told Tad about a speech the Prime Minister made. Every Sunday they spoke like this. The two of them laughed through their teeth. I tried to listen, but Llinos was arguing loudly with the boy in front of her.

'I heard your dog howling last night,' the boy said, the 's' whistling through the gap where his front teeth were growing stunted. 'My mam says your lot are lazy letting it carry on like that.'

'What's your mam got to do with anything?'

'I'm just telling you.'

The boy had small whales embroidered into his collar, rudimentary things his mother conjured, their mouths thick angry gaps.

'You're dirty,' I said to Llinos, before she could start arguing again. 'How did you manage to get dirty from the house to here?'

I spat on my thumb and rubbed her cheek. The boy turned back. I chided Llinos for arguing in chapel. She said she didn't understand why she shouldn't. I listened in to Tad's conversation, which had turned to lobster fishing, and Reverend Jones stood with his hands outstretched, his eyes closed, waiting for them to quiet.

~

Reverend Jones's sermon took its usual path. Prosperous fishing must be prayed for, a trade with a proper godly life, then the shipping forecast for the coming week. Sometimes his voice was drowned out by seagulls outside. He told the parable of the soils. I looked at the women in the other pews and ranked their hairstyles from best to worst. We crossed ourselves.

A still and calm sea, Lord, and a still and calm passage –

Bless the men who go freely into the darkness of the sea, so that we on the island may see light

I folded the material of my dress into a long concertina and let it fan out again.

I woke up when Reverend Jones introduced Edward, who had been sitting in the front pews without me noticing. Now that he was off the boat and not paled by seasickness I could see he was covered in dark freckles, and that his hair, no longer blown about by the wind, was straight and neat, dark copper, forming a line across the top of his head. He wore a yellow ascot, like a film star I'd seen in a magazine. He tried to speak in Welsh, but it was clumsy. He did not know the words for *stay*, *village*, or *house*. Joan sat silently next to him, writing something down in her lap. When the Reverend mentioned her, she turned and waved. I looked at the floor. For some reason, I did not want to be seen.

SJCEG Transcription 13 1.

A story told to island children. One day a little boy goes to the sand dunes to play. While there he notices a small finger-bone uncovered on the foreshore, and takes it home. He places it under his pillow. It is not supposed to be there – it is supposed to be underground. And because of the bone having been taken from its rightful spot, the world is flipped upside down. Fish begin to walk on land, sprouting legs, mouths gaping for air. Birds fall from the sky and begin crawling. Animals move down to the sea and begin to drown themselves. People walk on their hands. The trees heave themselves from the ground and stand on their roots like feet. Rabbits turn and hunt the foxes, butterflies hunt deer. The boy hears a voice, loud in his ears, from deep in the ground. The voice says, 'Give me back my bone!'

The boy is scared, and he goes immediately back to the dune, where he places the bone on the foreshore where he found it. He says a prayer to God, asks for forgiveness, asks for the world to be made right again. And he watches as the moon and sun switch back to their normal places, and the birds sing from the trees above his head.

Sometimes, when something else is knocked out of place, you see this upside-down world until balance is restored. If my father found a bird that couldn't fly, or found a dead sheep far out at sea, he would come home and pull my pockets inside out, because he was convinced I'd stolen something. Have you seen the whale down on the beach? My father would go lunatic.

Collected 12.10.38 from G. Stephens (Hound Breeder, b. 1873), residing Y Bwthyn Gwyn (White Cottage). Told to me on my first day, after a sermon, translated by the resident Baptist minister. Folktale Variation.

I thought of the English couple as the days changed, became colder, became darker, and as the grass turned sickly and brown. In herring season the long days turned slowly into each other, like a body moving in its sleep. The light took on a silver sheen in the morning and gut-red at dusk, and as the birds gathered closely to us on the shore, knowing that we put out fish there. Long tables were erected on the foreshore, catches spilling across them. The women who work there had nails dark with blood, aprons wiped with guts. I thought of the English couple wrinkling their nose at the damp smell, at the rust-sick boats.

Llinos and I had two buckets of cockles already and I was carrying more in my skirts, which had begun to sag and grow damp. Ahead of us, a horse dragged rakes through the sand to upturn the cockles and we followed behind it, looking for their white backs.

The wind was strong and thrashed the beach out of cover. On the sand were dry dune grasses that had been ripped up at the root. A stream of gulls followed us, picking at the sand fleas exposed in the tunnels left behind. Llinos turned and stood in front of me. I asked her what she was looking at, and she nodded at something behind me.

Joan was weaving between the long tables. She was chatting to the women, laughing. She wore a long beige coat. When she reached the outer edge of the tables, the women gesticulated down the beach, towards us. Joan saw me and smiled. We stood silently as she walked towards us, wrapping her coat against the wind.

When she reached us, she was out of breath. She held out her hand to me and greeted us by nodding her head.

'Cold, isn't it?'

'Nice to see you again.'

'Jolly nice,' Joan said.

She moved a frond of hair from her eyes with a bony, delicate finger. Her eyes were clear and bright.

'How is the project going?' I asked her. I could hear my heart in my ears.

'Barely started. We're just getting used to the weather.' She pointed to her cheeks, which were patterned with broken veins.

'Of course.'

'I've been looking for you. I went to your cottage but no one was in. I wondered if you might be interested in some work. It's good work. Secretarial.'

'Secretarial?'

'Writing, translating. My colleague and I are looking for someone. We were both impressed with you when we met you. You have good English, good Welsh.'

'Yes,' I said. I fiddled with the cockles in my skirt.

'Right. Well, perhaps we can talk more. Although I don't want to get in the way.'

'You wouldn't,' I said, quickly.

'I've heard you're a bit of a scholar.'

'I thought about training to be a teacher on the mainland. But my father needs me here for now.'

I suddenly became aware of my appearance, my wet skirt full of shells. I looked like an ordinary sort of peasant woman. I dropped the cockles onto the sand, asked Llinos to put them into the buckets. Llinos shot me a dark look, but obeyed.

I turned back to Joan.

'We can talk now,' I told her.

Joan smiled. Her eyes watered and ran. My breath steamed in front of me, merging all of her features into one blurred shape.

~

We sat in a windbreak, behind a cluster of rocks. Joan was amused by the sudden change in weather, how warm the air was without the wind.

'It's wonderful here,' she said, fanning her coat out underneath her. 'It's like another world. When I was a little girl, I was always imagining far-off places. There is a novel called *Treasure Island*—'

'I know *Treasure Island*,' I said. 'I've read it.'

Joan continued: how she had dreamt of a place untouched by cities, where the people were like wildflowers. I had never looked closely at the island. I had never thought it was interesting, or beautiful. We were quiet for a moment, and I looked at the beach, the tables, the women talking, the roofs of the houses on the cliffs. I thought I should tell Joan about spring, when wool is collected from the sheep and made into yarn. Fragments of wool escape and float on the air, like fairies' wings.

'It beats the city, certainly.'

'I'd love to go to the city.'

Joan laughed. 'Which one?'

'I hadn't thought that far ahead.'

Joan laughed again, harder. 'You're witty. I like witty women.'

'Have you ever been on a train?' I asked. She nodded.

'What was it like? Is it true that it screams?'

She told me all about it: the dining car, the green hills passing by the window, the way you put your suitcase on a rack above your head, and yes, the screaming. While she talked, I looked out at the horizon and imagined a boat was coming towards me, something golden and shining. When I looked back at her I saw the gold crucifix at Joan's collar, and the top button of her blouse made from imitation shell.

'I didn't know women could go to university on the mainland,' I said.

'Of course they can. They've been going for a while now.'

'What else can they do?'

'Most things. Why shouldn't they?'

I had no answer.

'Your English is perfect,' Joan said, watching me thoughtfully. 'Edward was worried we wouldn't find someone.'

'I learnt at school. From Sister Mary and from reading *Woman's Own*.'

She laughed loudly, again. I laughed too. No one found me funny on the island.

'I see. Well, it's perfect. You could pass for an English-woman.'

Joan looked out at the sea.

'Greatest country in the world.'

The western side of the island had a cave that the sun could not reach, hidden inside an overhanging cleft of rock. When it rained, the water gurgled and raced to get down there. When it was hot, the cave's dank smell reached over the island like a hand. Llinos said there was a creature living in the cave, a pure white eel with yellow eyes. She said one of the boys on the island had told her about it, that a gang of them had seen it in the shallow water one summer. I didn't believe it. I thought it was a mutation passed down, or a trick of cave-light on an ordinary eel. Still, there were times I thought about looking for it, bringing it back for her in a jar. I liked to imagine Llinos's face when she saw it. Llinos loved the island in ways that I did not. I liked to imagine Llinos's face reflected on the jar's surface, the white body curled inside the glass. The yellow eyes looking back at her.

I set up the tin bath in the yard. Heated a pan on the stove, and moved the water from inside to outside. The steam caught the plants and froze. Llinos climbed in first. Plunged her hands into the water with the soap. I saw fish scales rising to the surface.

'You haven't washed your hands properly,' I said.

'I have—'

'You're putting scales into the water.'

I pulled her hands out, then fished along the tub's base for the nailbrush. Llinos wriggled and splashed my clothes. I held her hands over the side of the tub and brushed the scales from them onto the ground, opal discs. She cried out that she was cold.

I brought her hands up to my mouth, and panted on them. Her hands smelt in a way I remembered from Mam's hands. I used to hate the smell. I wished that I could suck the smell off them, and spit it back into the sea.

~

Afterwards we sat in front of the fire inside to warm up, and to dry our wet hair. Tad was in the water outside, and I could hear his body moving, the water slopping over the sides. I told Llinos about my job with the couple.

'That Englishwoman,' Llinos said. 'She was strange.'

'Not really. You're just not used to people like that.'

'Like what?'

'People who aren't farmers or fishermen.'

She was holding yarn for me while I worked on an embroidery. I did not know what it was yet. I had made sheep on a hill and people, and was starting on a party of black crows.

'What did she ask you?'

'To help her. They're writing a book.'

'A book?'

'About the island. They're from the mainland. Way way across, in Oxford. They work for a university. Joan says we are very interesting. Reverend Jones told them about my English.'

'I know that. I was there—'

'They want to talk to people but they don't understand Welsh. Joan learnt a bit of Welsh but she says it's still like tongues. Joan is very funny.'

'What does she want to know about the island?'

'Everything, I suppose.'

My hands moved methodically, without me realising. I knotted the black yarn and started with green, to make small patches of dune grass.

'You should make that one a skeleton,' Llinos said.

She pointed at one of my crows, who looked to be lying on the ground.

'Pass me the white thread,' I said. I wanted to make it up to her after the cockles.

'Manod,' she said.

One white bone appeared over the black.

'Do you have hair on yourself? On your private areas?'

I started the spine, two ribs. Embroidering a straight line was easy.

'Yes, Llinos. All ladies have it.'

'Cadoc kept asking me if he could see it.'

I thought of Cadoc – the lanky farm boy in the west of the island, one of six sons.

'Don't show it to him.'

I let her nestle into me while I worked. I didn't have to go over my skeleton: the white thread showed up nicely against the black. I held the hoop at arm's length to see the whole scene. It looked as though the crows were gathered around the dead one. A funeral party, or a feast.

~

After Llinos had gone to bed I touched myself under my skirt. I lifted it and found the right fold and let myself feel the pleasure of it. I tried to think of Llew and the time we'd spent together, but all I could think about was Joan, her hands pink in the cold, and the way she rubbed at her watering eyes with her fingers, making them shine silver.

The herring were gathered in bwrws and dragged back onto the boats to be sold on the mainland. The women worked quickly, tying the bwrws together at the tail and then stringing them up onto one long wire. The younger women, fresh from school, tied short ribbons to the herrings' fins. On the mainland there were large murals on some of the buildings, advertising the island's herring: the herring were silver, and blue, and smiling, with neat ribbons around them in bright colours. Really, the ribbon was more like strips of sacking, and not as bright as the picture, and the herring looked brown and sad.

Rosslyn used to say that people on the mainland barely know the island is here: maybe they glimpse it on a clear day, but they don't think about it, and certainly don't think about visiting. Tad says, *They think about it when they have fish on their plates. They would think about it if there were no fish anymore. That's the last I'll hear about it, Elis. Manod. I said, Manod! Jesus Christ.*

In the mornings, I was supposed to go to the Saint pictures and pray. It was something Tad asked me to do. Reverend Jones said technically we were to have nothing to do with the Saints, but all of the fishermen did it. Supposedly St Brendan would stop them from being taken under by a wave. I always told him to not wear his rubber boots if he did not want to drown: those are the things that would drown him. I cleaned the hearth, opened the door and watched the ashes fall in spirals.

Joan was waiting for me outside the chapel. I wore my best clothes, a white muslin dress, and oiled my hair down. Joan greeted me and motioned me over to one of the chapel outhouses, where Edward was waiting.

Edward was reading at a wooden table. The outhouse had holes in the roof that dripped slowly, and a large iron door. Joan sat next to Edward, and motioned me to the empty chair opposite them. I looked across the table between us, a mess of papers, leather-bound notebooks, and a large black box with a brass clasp. Edward took a sheaf of paper from the top of the pile and handed it to me.

'Joan said she'd told you a bit about the project,' he said, without looking up. 'This just outlines the sort of things we want to find out.'

'Good morning,' I said, doing a small curtsey.

'I don't know why you wore white,' Edward said.

His eyes flickered to Joan, who ignored him.

'You'll need to wear something hardy in future.'

'Oh, Edward, show a little grace,' Joan said, smiling at me.

I took the paper from Edward's outstretched arm and read the list.

Food, custom.

Weddings, funerals.

Songs, tales.
Children's games.
Agriculture.
Special occasions.
Geography.
Chapel.

'It's a long list,' I said, looking up at them.

'We have a long time,' Joan said, smiling. 'We'll stay until the end of the year.'

'We're waiting for our equipment to arrive soon,' Edward said, reading over something. 'It was too heavy for the boat we came in. So for now we just want to plan what we're doing, and make some contacts. You'll have to translate for us. Oh, when does the post go out next?'

He looked up then, watched me over his glasses. His lips were large and chapped, and his breath misted up the lenses.

'I don't know. I think next month.'

'Next month?'

'It does not go very often. Might be next month, might be the month after that. You could send a telegram through the lighthouse but it's only for emergencies.'

Edward looked sharply at Joan and rolled his eyes.

'I'm going for a cigarette,' he said.

He knocked the table as he left, and the pile of papers slid off. I caught them, but not the pencil, which clattered on the stone floor.

'He hasn't slept since we arrived,' Joan said.

'He seemed so kind at my house. Did I upset him?'

She moved to my side of the table, and replaced the pencil.

'I'm sorry about the post,' I said.

'It's all right. It's hardly surprising. He's just keen to send letters back to our supervisor.'

'I'm sorry I wore white.' I felt as though I might cry.

'Would you like your picture taken?' Joan asked, her voice bright.

She reached for the large black case at the end of the table. She held it gently in one hand and with the other motioned for me to move my chair closer to her. *Closer, left, stop.* She told me to sit still.

I tucked my hair behind my ears. I held my hands in my lap one way, and then moved them to a different position, one on top of the other. I shuffled my feet together. I hadn't had my photograph taken since I was a baby, with the wooden horses. When the flash was released, my eyes were swarmed with vivid green spots, which lingered for the rest of the day.

My father was crouching over the bucket in the yard when I returned home, counting the lobsters he had collected. He had brought his cages close to the house, and they smelt like the inside of a cave, were crusted white. The glass floats lay around him like orbs. Elis sniffed around them, then pawed Tad's knee. He straightened up painfully.

'Watch how I count them. Copy me.'

I knelt to the bucket and kept it still between my knees. I watched my father move two lobsters at the top out by the tail, and hold them so they would not pinch him. I did the same, and counted the shells underneath quickly.

'Seven.'

'Are you speaking English at home now?'

'*Saith*.' It was not very many.

Behind him, the oil lamp. A tanker had come ashore on the island that spring, and the entire island was still using its cargo. Light flickered through the window. I could see sand in his beard. He had detached his tooth-plate and moved it from one side of his mouth to the other, with a clicking sound. I watched his hand. The fishing scars there reminded me of stitches, bone-white thread.

'I want to ask you something,' he said, sniffing. 'Are you working for the English couple?'

I nodded.

'Llinos told me.'

'They said I could go to university.'

'They say that war is coming. I don't know if being around the English is a good idea.'

I know who had told him: fishermen who shout when they pass Tad's boats, buyers on the mainland, newspapers that arrived intermittently and were so passed around the words were often smudged.

'It hasn't come yet,' I said.

I went inside before he could say anything else. Sat by the fire and listened to him carry the pail from one side of the yard to the other, cleaning the fish with the knife he kept in his boot, talking to Elis under his breath. I closed my eyes and saw his eyes looking back at me, pale as clear water.

In bed, I imagined I could hear Edward and Joan writing through the wall. I closed my eyes and felt Llinos's heat next to me, her ribcage rising and dropping. Elis skittered across the floor in the next room. I imagined the sound of their pens on paper, pencil tracing over their words, my words, as I translated them, until these imaginings merged with the sounds of seagulls in their night-flying over the roof, the slap of their feet as they landed.

Different colours on the surface of the sea meant different things. Black – storm coming. Colour of shit – a good day for boats.

There was a year when the sea turned to ice for half a mile around the edge of the island. A dreadful winter. In the chapel Reverend Jones stared blankly back at us, as though he did not want to think about what it meant. Most of Merionn's sheep were killed for food, and the rest froze to death. The sheep he has now are descended from the three who survived.

Trees came to shore in their hundreds during one of the storms and the men built coffins for themselves, their wives and children. When spring came and it was like a miracle, they turned them upside down and used them for boats, and for carrying fish back to the shore.

If a jellyfish was washed up, someone was keeping a secret.

If the water was covered in petrels, the morning would bring frost.

I gathered a few fishermen to sing the songs they sing on the boats. I offered them some of the money Joan had given me, a few pennies and cigarettes, and led them from the beach up to the chapel where Joan and Edward were waiting.

When they started to sing, their voices echoed up to the roof. Against the men, Edward looked very tall and very pale, with a white and red mouth like a kitten.

Edward asked me to translate the lyrics of the song, while he listened. He wrote down the notes of the music. I had never seen music written that way before. I knew the song by heart and finished writing it down quickly. I watched Edward. He looked intently at the men.

The altar was rudimentary, covered by an old shawl, and behind it was a mural of ugly saints and fishing boats. I had painted over a section when I was a child, a group of us tasked with brightening the dulled colours. Reverend Jones had chosen us girls for our steady hands and neat handwriting. I remember painting over a horse in dark red. It had a wild, heavy face. I had asked the Reverend if I really did have to paint over each hair of its long, red mane and he had said, why wouldn't you? He believed we owed a great debt to the people who had first painted on the wall. Rosslyn had been next to me, repainting smaller things: fish, lizards, birds. Afterwards we looked at the different figures and ran our fingers over them. People dancing and holding hands. A yellow moon. A man wearing a mask resembling a bird we didn't know, the beak long and curved.

The song was about a shipwreck, a fishing boat lost at sea. When the men were finished, Edward asked me about the seals that appeared in the song. They are a metaphor, he said, aren't they, for the dead sailors washed up onto the beach in the last verse? And I told him no, they are two separate things.

It was a hâf bach, a little summer, the sun roosting for a few days on the turn of autumn. Seals brought their children to the shore. The pups were white and fluffy, and I took Llinos to see them. There was a bull, fat as a legless cow. It was far away enough that it would not catch up with us if it charged. We played a clapping game until one of the baby seal pups sidled up to us. Llinos cooed over it, and patted its head. For some reason, it was unafraid. Behind it, another was suckling on a rock for comfort. We walked home through the dunes, Llinos picking sand sedge from the ground. She held a bunch to me, and asked if I thought it smelled like a horse's mouth.

SJCEG Transcription 20.

The woman took the seal pup and raised it as her own. That's the end of the story my grandmother told me, though I can't remember the rest. I just remember the ending. I do remember parts – the woman had a son, and the son drowned. That's right. And the son came back as the seal, for some reason. And the woman took the seal in, fed it from her breast. I remember that. I wanted to be a seal pup. And stay with my mother.

Collected 12.10.38 from D. Evans (Boat Builder, b. 1900), residing Atty Draw (Double House, name m. 'Over There').

Cold fell, left a thin layer of frost on the ground. The whale's body seemed to dry out, the edges of its mouth becoming ragged. The smell collapsed over us.

Edward's equipment arrived and I collected it from the shore. I had to borrow a wheelbarrow from Leah. Two men brought a large suitcase through the shallows, a narrow wooden box, and a coil of wire. They placed it on the ground in front of me. I paid them and waited as they counted the money.

'Do you live here?' one of the men asked. 'I've heard a lot of things about this island.'

I took a closer look at him. He was thin, scrawny, with dark teeth and a smattering of angry red spots across his nose.

'Have you now?' I said.

'Why don't you move to the mainland? You could get work. Warmer than here and nicer houses. You could get a nice husband, too.'

I pulled my scarf tighter around my shoulders and watched the seals at the edge of the beach, their stone bodies. The men climbed back into their boat and left, the waves pushing one end of their boat higher and higher. The seals followed them and disappeared beneath the water.

Edward placed the suitcase on the table and opened it, revealing a recording machine. He beckoned me over to look.

'This is a phonograph,' he explained, excitedly. 'But – disc recording. Not cylinders, which are easily wasted. Better quality sound. World-class. Better for transporting. See? Professor John – my colleague, he recommended it, twisted the bursar's arm for funding.'

'We don't have a word for it.'

'Of course you don't. Why would you?'

Wanting to be helpful, I opened the narrower case, and found it full of thin black discs. I ran my finger over them. Edward pulled the box away from me, and shut it.

'It's rather important that we look after the equipment.'

He unpacked a small round microphone, and set it on the table. I picked it up, and the wire knocked heavily against the table. I apologised under my breath and placed it back down.

I watched Edward closely. His hands moved quickly and gently. He pulled out one of the black discs and inspected both sides, bringing it up to his eye-level. He placed it into the machine and lowered a small arm onto its surface.

'Shall we test it out?' he asked me.

'OK,' I said.

'Would you like to sing something?'

'I could.'

I sang a few lines of something Mam used to sing to us, a song about love. Edward moved the microphone closer to me. He gestured to me to continue.

'You have a beautiful voice,' he said when I finished. The disc kept spinning, emitting a velvety rustle.

'Thank you.'

'I sing too,' Edward said. 'I came to my college on a choral scholarship. I had to sing in the college chapel every day.'

I wanted to ask more but Joan entered with two books in her hands, and placed them on the table without looking at us. Edward started messing with the machine again. He was blushing.

'With this you don't have to stay for all of the interviews,' Edward said. 'You can just help us translate afterwards.'

'Yes!' agreed Joan. 'Also, Manod – I wanted to ask you to take me around the island. Show me a few places.'

I nodded, and said the word 'microphone' under my breath until it stopped sounding like a word.

~

I saw Olwen as Joan and I left. She was a year older than me and recently married. Her belly high and tight under her clothes. I smiled at her and she smiled back. I watched her walk away, her ankles pink where they appeared

77

beneath her skirt. She met her husband at the end of the path, and he walked ahead of her without looking back. I'd seen girls married at sixteen, with children by twenty, widowed by the sea by twenty-five, worn out and lost.

SJCEG Disc 1A.

I<small>F</small> <small>MY LOVE</small> comes to our door,
If my love comes to tap the grey window pane,
Answer him politely, give a kind reply,
Tell him I am not home, I do not wish to be home,
A man from another place has taken me away,
A man from another place has taken me away,
Tonight, here tonight, if my love answers,
Tell him the sea moves faster than the wind.

*Collected 24.10.38 from M. Llan (b. 1920), residing Y Bwthyn
Rhosyn (Rose Cottage). Folk song.*

My Baptist host shows me the island records. He writes them himself every Christmas. He says it does not account for everyone, as some are lost at sea every year or so.

The island population has been declining since the turn of the century. Many move to the mainland in search of a more stable income, particularly in the younger generations. Most of the young people left are young women awaiting marriage, with a handful of young men taking up their fathers' fishing trades. I ask my host how concerned he is about this and he says, very. He tries to teach the virtues of the homestead in his sermons, for the young women to remain in the home on the island and for young men to stay. But it is difficult, he says, when the weather is so rough, and making a living so difficult. You can't blame them for wanting to leave it behind.

A boat returned that evening. A herring boat. One man from the island and a crew of other fishermen who would sail on the following morning. They were staying at the lighthouse. Tad made us visit, in case they had brought whiskey or newspapers.

One of the men cornered me. I didn't recognise him, and he said he was from Denmark. His tongue had a thin white froth running over it. He told me a story about a young man who died at sea, on the boat they had come in on. They had been playing cards, as they did most nights to pass the time. The man had laid his cards down without speaking, then ran across the deck and threw himself into the sea. By the time the boat could stop and turn back, he had disappeared. He didn't seem to want a response to the story, just to tell it. I excused myself and slipped away from him.

On the other side of the room, Llinos sat on Tad's lap. Tad had his arm snaked around her, holding his drink. She was asleep, bobbing up and down as Tad talked to the man next to him. They shared a newspaper. *5,000 British Troops Sent to Sudetenland*, read the front page. A photograph of Neville Chamberlain, his arms outstretched. Three weeks out of date.

The man from Denmark kept talking very close to my face, and his breath stank like a dog. I walked over and took

Llinos, so that I could go home. She murmured as I picked her up, and threaded her arms around my neck. She said something in her sleep, something about jam. I said to her, Tell me all about it tomorrow.

On her good days, Mam would wake us up by climbing into the bed with us. We would drift in and out of sleep together. She told us her favourite stories, scenes from her life. Birds throwing shadows beyond the window. She had not grown up on the island but on the mainland coast, on her father's farm. She had three brothers. In harsh winters, they taught her how to hunt partridge and small game. Once, she had set snares for rabbits, not realising she had strayed into the neighbouring farmer's field. Her father called her to the front step one morning, where her brothers were waiting for her. Seven rabbits had been left against the farmhouse door, their feet tied with the red wire of the traps. Their bodies had been cut open and doused with urine by the neighbour, so they were inedible. Her brothers did not speak to her for a week.

I was not suited to that life, she always said, at the end of it. *I couldn't read that land like my brothers did.* Sometimes she added, *There's no job for a woman to get except wife.*

I wondered how she felt coming here, realising the island was one long farm, the sea shifting the edges of the fields. Under the covers she held our bodies tightly, leaving red welts.

Part of the whale's insides emerged onto the sand, petals of fat blue and mauve. Blood spread across the tideline. The birds continued to carve chunks out of its back. High tide brought the whale back out to deeper waters, where fish attached themselves to the edges of the body like frills, and low tide returned it, a bed of insects cushioning its chin.

The wind had swept sea-mist up onto the cliffs. The air was damp, late morning light. Skeletal remains of old houses. Water and salt marsh as far as you could see. Ferns along the tops of the cliffs, their fronds beginning to disintegrate. Joan wanted to see the cliffs, and wrote down everything I told her.

We passed an old tyre left to rot. I pointed it out to Joan, explained how we always find washed-up parts of the Great War here. Uniforms, helmets. Shards of naval mines. Once a live grenade. Llinos and I hid in the house while the island adults waited for soldiers to arrive on the foreshore.

Joan did more talking than looking, and she wrote a lot of things down in a looping scrawl I couldn't decipher. She told me about her father's country house and the racing pigeons he bred there. She spoke about them with great tenderness, their silver and fawn-freckled feathers and snow-white bouffant chests. I had never seen a racing pigeon and so I listened closely to her description. Joan said they are the size of a kitten. I thought it was enchanting. I wondered what they did with the bird shit, but kept it to myself.

'Of course, they are terribly clever animals, pigeons.'

I recognised some of the words she was writing: cliff, gull, egg.

'They took messages during the Great War. Knew exactly where they were going.'

I did not answer. I had to guide Joan over the ground, the potted rabbit burrows, sea thrift and bare patches of earth. Most of the eggs had already been collected. I crouched down and showed her where the grass had been matted into nests, pieces of shell left behind by adders, boot-prints of the people who got there before us.

When I stood, Joan was distracted.

'I love the sea,' she said, nodding to where it rose up over the land's edge. 'It's romantic, don't you think?'

I didn't think.

'Those white things are boats,' I said, pointing out the dots in the distance. 'One of them will be my Tad. Collecting lobster.'

'Your father is a lobster fisherman?'

I nodded. Joan seemed delighted.

'We must talk to him. Are there many lobster fishermen on the island?'

'Three. My father and two others.'

We watched the boats for a while, rowing slowly through the water. I felt the hem of Joan's coat touch my arm. When Tad returned, I knew he would stink of salt, of fish blood, but now the boats looked tiny and delicate against the vast sea, like granules of sugar across a tablecloth.

'There aren't many young people,' Joan said thoughtfully. 'Like you.'

'They've gone—'

I felt my ankle twist and drop at an angle, and cried out. I had not been looking, and it had dropped into a rabbit burrow. The pain was clean and sharp, and when Joan helped me up my ankle felt warm, as though a hand was wrapped around it, slowly getting tighter.

~

It took us a long time to get back down to the beach. I struggled to lean on my ankle, and Joan tried to carry me but was not strong enough. I felt embarrassed and tried to distract her. I pointed out where you could see the mainland, the faded gathering of roofs. The small pink flowers in the grass which would stay until the first frost. Joan stopped and made notes silently. I told her that I was named after a kind of coastal herb. It was a lie, but I was nervous and wanted to impress her.

'Are you married?' I asked her, eventually.

'Oh, no.' She laughed. 'I'm far too busy for that.'

'Busy doing what?'

'Writing, reading, speaking, eating, sleeping.'

'I didn't know you could do that.'

'Do what?'

'Just . . . not get married.'

She nodded, uninterested. We stopped walking while she made a note of something. I peered at the page. *Small winding footpaths over the cliffs*, it said. *Very cold on beach. M seems used to it.*

'What will you call the book?' I asked.

She smiled. 'I'm thinking something like, Stories from the Edge-lands.'

'I like it.'

'Edward wanted something more ethereal, like Stories of a Disappearing Class.'

'Are we disappearing?'

Joan bent down to pick some flowers and small shoots, and trapped them in her notebook. I told her the names: bladder campion, vernal squill. She dusted herself down. There was nothing there.

'Well,' she said, clearing her throat. 'The island has already lost a lot of people. At the turn of the century?'

'Did Reverend Jones tell you that?'

She nodded.

'A lot of the mainlanders started coming over, buying up the houses,' I told her. 'This was all before I was born. But Tad tells me. The houses were cheap.'

'But they didn't stay?'

'Too isolated and too cold, apparently. They went back. The islanders got the idea they should go too. I don't blame them.'

'Would you like to leave?'

A gull came close to my foot, and I kicked out at it,

feeling a stab of pain. It moved away, frozen, its beak open in defence.

'I can't leave Llinos.'

The wind picked up, blowing sand over our shoes.

'I shall interpret that as a yes,' Joan said, before walking on.

I stayed for a few moments. My cheek felt itchy, and I rubbed it against my collar. I heard the gull crying to its friends. There were clouds on the horizon the same colour as the sea. A boat disappeared beyond it, as though falling off a sharp edge.

~

We passed a group of women on the way back, collecting cockles before the tide came in. Wives of fishermen loading up carts with boxes of fish. Joan kept taking off her gloves to run her fingers over the fish in the trays. The women shouted commands to each other.

There was a knocking sound as the shells hit the buckets. Joan stopped and watched them, mesmerised. One of the women came over to us, an old woman, in a purple shawl. She grabbed my hands and pressed them, and I pulled them roughly away.

'It's truly amazing,' Joan said. 'The way you live.'

I watched the sea behind us, the way it roughly moved, mutated. There was a boat on the shore, with a small boy inside of it. He was the son of Tad's friend. The boy's uncle had drowned at sea, and the boy became terrified of the water. His father took him out in the boat every morning and evening, so the child would no longer be afraid, and could grow to be a fisherman. The boy fiddled with something in his lap, something no one else could see.

At home, Tad was sitting by the fire, slowly falling asleep. He started awake when I opened the door. Asked me if it was dark outside. Getting there, I told him.

'They shouldn't be keeping you out so late,' he said, closing his eyes again.

I looked at the lobster bucket by the door, which today only held three. Not enough to eat, not enough to sell. I knew Tad did not approve of my studying. He had told me so, asking me again about Marc and his interest in me. But what I couldn't say is that Llinos and I couldn't rely on him, not anymore. I tied a sheet of muslin around my ankle, let it rest. By morning the pain was almost gone.

There was often talk of evacuation on the island. Sometimes council men from the mainland would arrive, ask us questions at the door. Did we know what earnings were on the mainland? Did we need help finding work there? Had the weather changed? They spoke a language we already knew: of weather, of rising water, of unnecessary hardship. We heard other stories, elsewhere: of families crammed into one room in terrace houses, of smog, conscription.

It had happened to other villages. A knock on the door. The villages made way for new collieries, landlords renting fields back to farmers, coastal resorts. One village near to us on the mainland became a golf course. Sometimes, I imagined I could see it, standing on my toes on the highest cliff on a clear day. I could see in my mind the swathes of green and the little red flags, women in yellow twinsets and their older husbands. I tried to imagine what they talked about, but could not.

I knew where I would go if an evacuation order came. I knew the people on the island who had relatives on the mainland, in the cities, in England, in Ireland, in America. I also knew the people who would have to stay behind.

I had planned it, in my head. I had recurring dreams about it. Tad would go to Llandudno to live with his uncle, the butcher. I would take Llinos out of the house and up the hill, along the path that wound along the sea. In summer the water looks like a polished floor, like you could skid across it. The ground shows up the footprints of cattle and sheep. There is a very large hill and cliff at the island's westernmost point, where no one really goes because the birds nest there all crammed together, and the rock is covered in a thick white layer of shit, and God knows how many skeletons of seagulls and mice.

I would look out towards the mainland and wait for the boat to pick us up. I would tie a hat onto my head at my chin. I did not own a hat like this, but thought maybe I would by then. On the boat a handsome sailor would see me, and welcome us aboard. The sailor would turn out to be rich. Llinos and I would travel across the sea with him like a gigantic fish, showing its belly to the sky.

The uncertainty of getting to the mainland dominates life on the island, the journey being around five miles in good weather, and over ten in bad.

The islanders seem very remote from the mainland. News comes in fragments. Only a handful knew an accurate timeline of recent events. Most of the islanders we spoke to asked if we had brought newspapers with us from the mainland. Many asked us questions about the possibility of war. One elderly woman, whose husband had been killed during a submarine attack in the Great War, asked us what we personally were planning to do about Adolf Hitler.

~

At the end of the school week, the children play on the beach, until it is too cold and their mothers call them in. A great variety of amusing games, some active and some sedentary, interspersed with nursery rhymes and songs.

Omitting universal games such as football, Hopscotch, Leap Frog, marbles etc., we observe: All the Birds in the Air and All the Fishes in the Sea, Brandy Wicket, Blind Hob, Cat and Mouse, Crab King, Five Stones, East Wind West Wind, Honey Pot, Hide and Find, Jib Job Jeremiah, Mabel Mabel, Magpie Catcher, Rabbit Pie, Seal Chaser, Three Jolly Butchers, and Weaving Needles.

Most of the games involve animals, chasing, and plucking crabs from rock pools. When evening comes, and sheep move down to the beach to eat seaweed, the games shift to involve the sheep as shields, obstacles, or unwilling listeners. The sheep are especially noisy at these times. It is striking how similar they sound against the children.

Do you ever want to leave the island? I asked Llinos when
we were side by side in bed.

Ydych chi erioed eisiau gadael yr ynys?

No, Llinos said, without opening her eyes.

Na dwi ddim.

I could teach you some more English.

Fe allwn i ddysgu mwy o Saesneg i chi.

I don't need English here.

Dwi ddim angen Saesneg yma.

I pulled a stray piece of straw from her pillow.

Joan says this place is charming.

Dywed Joan fod yr ynys yn swynol.

What does she mean?

Beth mae hynny'n ei olygu?

I rip out another straw.

I don't know. I think it's a good thing.

Dydw i ddim yn gwybod. Rwy'n meddwl ei fod yn beth da.

The next day, Joan handed me a piece of paper as I arrived at the chapel. I unfolded it, and in the middle of the page was a painting she had made of a racing pigeon. It was completely different to how I imagined. The difference made me want to cry.

Mam always said that she had seen a spirit on the day Llinos was born. It was winter, the ground rock-hard with frost, mist hanging like a sail. She had been in the house kneading dough. Mam said she felt her stomach clench, and she doubled over, let her forehead cool against the stone floor. She does not remember how much time passed but when she unfurled herself her skirt was wet and she had a fever. She went to the window to cool her forehead on the glass. The window overlooked a dirt path heading down to the beach, which she could see a small part of. The beach was not sandy there, not like the other coves on the island, but covered with dark rocks slippery with weed.

Mam watched as one of the rocks opened up and something came out, a long shape that was yellow like the inside of an egg. It became the shape of a girl.

~

At some point after Llinos was born, Mam got smaller, thinner. She stopped venturing beyond the yard, apart from on Sundays to attend chapel, where she hovered, panting, in the pews. She stayed in bed most days, sleeping or lying with her eyes cold and open. Sometimes she came into the kitchen, stood next to us in silence for a few minutes, then returned to bed.

We took her to the doctor on the mainland, once, when Llinos was a year old and I was seven. The water was dark and choppy. Tad rowed, and I sat behind him, twisted round so that I could watch the red and white houses of the mainland come into view. I remember seeing nothing beneath the water, though Llinos swears she saw an eel lip the side of the boat.

Mam stayed in the doctor's for one hour. Tad waited with us outside. I remember people staring at me. A man told me I looked like Queen Victoria. A woman in the chair next to us offered Llinos and me a green grape each, and Tad had taken them gratefully for us but hidden them in his pocket, not knowing what exactly they were. Mam came out of the room, then, with a small bottle of round pink pills.

Tad had missed a day of fishing to take Mam to the mainland and so we ate from cans for supper: syrupy fruit, dry corned beef, stale bread. After eating Mam placed her knife and fork either side of her plate, and said that on receiving the bottle of pills she had experienced a vision. The Angel Gabriel had come to her and opened up her back with his sword, let out two wings. *Ac felly yr wyf yn gadwedig. Yr wyf yn gadwedig.* And so I am saved, she said. I am saved.

November

For a while we mourned the whale's body, its early signs of rot. Someone brought flowers, placed their coat over its back. The coat looked comically small, like a doll's apron. The smell worsened, stung our eyes. A dark cloud of gulls hovered over the beach. When they came towards the houses, they were potbellied and smug, shrieking like children. At night the sound of puffins, migrating late, out from their burrows in the hill. Llinos saw one in the window one night, its body almost white against the bushes. The whale was left pockmarked, and two of its ribs began to emerge.

Tad brought rubber gloves to protect my hands while I sorted through the lobsters he had caught. It was the last catch before winter. The lamplight turned darker and darker, until it smouldered with a tiny amber flame.

'Need paraffin,' Tad said.

'I'll ask around,' I said.

The fingers of the gloves were rough and white, with something that had dried slowly over time.

I weighed each lobster and wrote down the weight, and Tad would tell me a price to write next to it. He sat gutting dogfish, which he had started catching alongside the lobster. We didn't talk about this. Joan said that dogfish skin was used to sand down violins. The meat was tough and unpleasant to eat. Llinos sat next to us, watching Tad closely, picking the odd small bone from the bucket and holding it to the low light.

'Are you enjoying your job?' he asked me, without looking up.

He dragged a new basket of the fish over to his feet, plucked a dogfish, and struck a blow to its wriggling head. Dark liquid splattered against the knee of his trousers. He plunged his knife into it, plucking out the heart, which he threw to one side, for Elis to catch. It struck me that he had never gutted dogfish before, and yet still knew how to do it. I watched him work.

'Do you enjoy yours?'

'Why do you ask me that?'

'I was just curious. You have a knack with the dogfish.'

He looked over to me.

'I saw a fight on my way back from the mainland. I went to the docks. There was a crowd of men, ringed around two men fighting each other. Old men, my age. One of them used to work the market. I recognised him. The man next to me was taking bets and asked if I wanted one. I must have looked at him funny because he took offence. Said, It's honest work. Honest work. It's not a good sign, is it? Means they've no fish to sell. To be doing that.'

The rain fell against the window, making us jump. I fed food scraps to Elis, who knocked over one of the lobster cages, rattling open the door.

'Don't let it escape!' Tad cried.

The lobster sat dazed on the wooden floor. It waved its antennae lazily. I picked it up and turned it over, so it wouldn't nip me.

Most of the whale's fat had by now been eaten by birds and small fish in the water. Of the skin that was left, there were pockmarks and large scratches. For a long time, the children had pretended the body was a beached submarine, collecting driftwood to act as weapons against imaginary traitors inside, but now the tough black skin had retreated from the bones the game had lost its appeal.

The children brought flowers and grasses and placed them around the body. They held their faces in the crook of their elbows against the smell. One of the children, Cadoc, was dared to place them over the whale's cavernous head, but something cried out as he did so, and it startled him, so the flowers ended up lower down, over the whale's nose. Most of the children laughed and ran away. Llinos stayed, picked up the flowers, and moved them to where they were supposed to be. Over the days the whale turned paler, its skin tightening and coming away from the body, as if disappearing into the new-season light.

Joan wore red lipstick and had coloured her cheeks a bright pink. She stooped when she stepped inside the house. She told me she liked my outfit, a long velvet dress with a large bow on the rump.

'Turn around!' she cried. 'You look like something out of Dickens. Or the pictures. Some beautiful young heroine.'

I thanked her, and behind her head Tad raised his eyebrows and mouthed PARAFFIN. It had been the only way I could convince him to invite them both to dinner.

'You do look lovely, Manod,' Edward said, handing me a bottle of whiskey they had brought with them.

I waved him away. I was so pleased that Joan had complimented me. I was sick of the way she always saw me: my hair wet and plastered to my head, my skin dry and blotched, my skirt battered with dirt and sand from our walks.

~

Joan shrieked like a child when I put out the lobster meal. I had crushed the meat with oats into a paste, added herbs from the cliffs, and cooked potatoes on the side. I had taken some of Leah's goat butter, used pounds of it without realising.

'We've been eating corned beef and scrawny little potatoes.'

'We do usually eat that,' Tad said, flatly.

'In winter,' I added.

'But this is wonderful food. Better than I've ever had.'

I asked her if she cooked at home, and she chuckled.

'No, no. We always had staff for that. Nice girls, really. Always getting in the family way.'

She turned to my father.

'You must be proud of Manod. She is a very bright girl.'

'A wonderful singer,' said Edward.

Tad pointed to one of my embroideries which he had hung on the wall. A beach, a horse, a cart. A woman wrapped in her winter clothes, a lobster cage at her feet.

'Wonderful,' said Edward.

I flinched, and a hard bit of shell got stuck in my teeth. I felt my cheeks burn as everyone looked at me. I changed the subject.

'Joan is really enjoying the island, Tad.'

'Oh yes,' said Joan. 'It's quite wonderful. I love the nature here. Manod has been showing me the flowers. I love watching you all come in and out of the sea. Such a wonderful way to live.'

'Not easy.'

'Not easy,' Joan said softly. 'But worthwhile. Honest. Truly, how humans are supposed to live. In tune with nature.'

Edward coughed. Our eyes met over the table. I could not read his expression.

'I get it from my father,' Joan continued. 'My love of nature. My father loved trees. He cultivated orchards and woodland over most of my family's land. He kept an army of potted saplings in the courtyard. He would go out with his binoculars for most of the week and return covered in dirt, with a list of birds as long as his arm. He would sell the wood to the army but always plant more trees again. Isn't that special? No one else was doing it, you know. He truly understood the need for preserving woodland, the English landscape. Tell me.' She jabbed her knife at Tad's plate. 'Do you not feel rotten when you eat that lobster?'

I held my breath. Tad did not answer. I looked up at Joan. She smiled at me. Her front teeth were spotted with the lipstick, and I motioned to her to wipe it off. She dabbed at her teeth with her napkin and left a pink smear behind.

'Not when the alternative is corned beef, I imagine,' Edward said, smiling.

Tad took out his tooth-plate and placed it on the table next to him. It did cause him trouble at mealtimes. He had kept it in to be polite, as without it his speech was difficult to understand. I knew this meant he wouldn't talk again unless necessary. Joan watched the tooth-plate intently, as though it might jump towards her.

'I've told some friends of mine about the island,

actually. About the whale,' Joan said. 'They collect things for the army. Whale oil, blubber. Wouldn't it feel rather pleasant for the body not to go to waste?'

No one answered.

'Shall we drink?' Edward said, breaking the silence.

I poured a round. The alcohol was sour and burned my throat. For some reason, I felt annoyed. The idea of the whale being taken. I ate the bread at the centre of the table until my stomach felt heavy and tight, until the lights swam across my eyes, making me feel dizzy.

~

I walked Joan and Edward back to their lodgings when the rain stopped. Tad mimed 'PARAFFIN' to me while they were putting on their coats.

The chapel looked ghostly at night. The windows reflected the grey sky. There was a line of green discs floating at the edge of the next field, the eyes of cows thronging there. Joan stayed by the door while Edward went inside to light the fire.

'I want to be honest,' she said, leaning against the stone wall.

Her words were slurring a little. I looked at a small silver filling in the back of her mouth.

'I want to be honest. I see much of myself in you. You are very bright, but to be a bright woman is . . . not always easy.'

She tilted her head, waiting for me to speak. I was not sure what she wanted me to say, and my vision felt blurred.

'My father died while I was an undergraduate. It is not the done thing for women to study and work but he wanted me to. Always paid for the best education he could for me. Then he died. I feel my work is indebted to him.'

One of the cows cried out. I thought I could see its breath erupt, its fawn-coloured ear.

'I would love to study. Like you,' I said quietly.

'I'm saying that you can. You must.'

I was struck by an image of myself in a quiet, light-filled room. Small trinkets on the mantelpiece. A space ready for Llinos.

'I know your mother died too,' Joan said. 'One of the women told me.'

She clasped my hand. Her hands felt wet and cold.

'They said she fell into the water.'

I pulled my hands away.

'We need paraffin,' I said. 'Do you have any spare?'

She disappeared inside for a minute, then emerged with a square red tin. She wanted to talk more, but I walked away quickly. When I was out of sight, I thought about pouring the bottle away, watching it spread across the rocks. I held the tin close to me, and instead counted the tears on my cheekbone, hot and quiet.

I woke up at dawn with a dry mouth. I stumbled to the outhouse and vomited. When I came back inside Tad was leaving for the boats, Elis worrying at his feet. The sun cast shimmering orange squares on the wall which made me feel nauseous again. I looked at myself in the mirror, my puffy eyes, the dark half-moons beneath them. I remembered pulling my hands away from Joan's, and groaned. A knot of guilt burrowed into my stomach, and made a nest there.

Edward invited me to sing most days. I arrived an hour before Joan, and he had coffee and milk waiting for me.

He would have sheet music on the desk for me to sing, but he would have to sing it first as I couldn't read it. He said a lot of things about music I didn't understand. Keys and instruments and songs I hadn't heard of. I would sing after him, and he would record it. Even in the rain I went, even when I arrived soaking, and had to sing through my blocked nose, my shivering. I liked the thoughtful way he looked at me, the way he nodded his head, folded his hands together in his lap. Sometimes he closed his eyes while I sang and my whole body felt it. I felt myself come out of my body, my body built for farming and fishing and having a farmer-fisherman's children, and float against the ceiling.

That day I sang even though my throat hurt, and I couldn't open my eyes against the sunlight.

Small bird, small bird
Where have you been?
Small bird, small bird
Where are you going?
Stay in my sight
Along the hill, along the path
Stay near to my feet
Small bird, small bird –

Edward waved at me to stop.

'All right, all right,' he said. 'We're both feeling delicate.'

I sat down at the table while he slowed the disc to a stop, and removed it from the machine. Edward had newspapers sent from the mainland, which he collected from Reverend Jones. He would let me read them most days. They were strewn across the table, and I picked one up at random.

'I liked your embroidery,' Edward said. 'On the wall. Do you have more?'

'Yes,' I said, moving the broad pages.

'I'd like to see them.'

'All right.'

I turned back to my newspaper. I was reading about a woman who had gone missing on the mainland. She was six foot tall and older than me. Her mother had reported her missing. The woman had apparently told her that she wanted to see the West End of London. See a bit of life. I felt Edward looking at me.

'Are you worried about a war?' he asked. His glasses reflected the window and the scene outside, long planes of green across his eyes and brow. 'You've been reading that article for a long time.'

Across the page was an article about Jewish children being banned from school in Germany.

'I don't know.' I wasn't lying. 'Should I be?'

'It probably wouldn't reach you here.'

'In the last war, the men all had to leave the island to

fight. The women were left behind and had to farm and fish themselves.'

'Like Lesbos,' he said, laughing. 'Sounds idyllic.'

'I hope to be long gone by then.'

Edward removed his glasses, and began polishing them with the sleeve of his jumper.

'I was seven when the war broke out,' he said. 'My father was too old to fight but my uncle went. My mother's twin brother. He came back very different, and with only half a nose. I don't know why I'm telling you that.'

'Because we were talking about the war.'

'Yes. Right.'

'What did you sing in the choir?'

'Hymns mostly. It was just in my college. I loved singing "Awake, Glad Soul". Do you know it?'

Outside the light had turned yellow. The birds had fallen silent, I realised. Edward coughed, and sat down beside me. He sang quietly, a song about Christ and spring. His hand was next to my hand, not touching it but very close. I could smell his breath, his laundry soap. I thought of him singing at his college. Then of the woman, her wish to see a bit of life. Edward started telling me that he had grown up in a vicarage, in the countryside. That his father believed that all birds were holy. I laughed. Behind us, the door opened and Joan walked in. Edward jerked his hand away.

Fishing on the island revolves primarily, charmingly, around lobster. Small wooden boathouses, storws, are clustered on each beach, and each of them filled with all manner of cages, glass and wooden floats, putrid-smelling gloves, and buckets for bait.

The fishermen say that to have a woman on a fishing boat is a curse; the same applying to a lost hare, or a corpse. Still, with some persuasion I am permitted to accompany a night collection, on a warmer evening when the water is still.

The craft is extraordinary: the traps are laid behind the lighthouse, so once out in the water it is pitch-dark. Only the sound of slopping water, and men clearing their throats. The men find their floats and pull up their charges blindly, as though in a dream. Their movements are balletic, supremely graceful, and accurate. They pile the rancid cages behind them in neat stacks.

Watching them, I am reminded of my brother, learning to empty and reload a rifle while blindfolded. The strength and guile of our countrymen, from all corners of the Isles.

Writing on the whale's body, which appeared over many days. The marks sank deep into the skin, which could not heal itself, and left pale markings.

Jacob, here

A heart

Three penises

Six sets of initials: H.S&C.G, L.E&F.J, G.B&E.S.

An unnatural indentation, the print of a small thumb.

The island was showered in a thin white frost. The waves tipped over themselves. Wind crushing the grass. The cliffs became full of birds in their fat winter feathers, their black eyes peeping. Edward brought newspapers to the house for Tad to read, which he had been sent the week before. *There is No New Crisis at Present*, announced one of the headlines.

Tad told me to teach Llinos household matters, to keep her inside the house. Llinos pretended she did not hear my instructions and sat on the floor, laying out small stones and then scooping them up with her hand. *Dwi'n pysgod*, she said. I'm fishing.

Later I found the door open slightly and a trail of footprints leading out. Llinos was crouched in a patch of shingle half a mile from the cottage, the wind blowing her skirt out to one side, her head down. She picked out clams from the ground, cleaned them on her collar and dropped them into a bucket next to her.

'Look, Manod,' she said, when I reached her. 'See how close they come to the house.'

That night Tad returned with his biggest catch all season, a school of bull huss that he claimed jumped freely into his lap. The catch was so large that another fisherman,

Dai, had to help him carry it home, and when he crossed the threshold said, *The little girl wasn't there. When she's on the beach we catch nothing.*

Joan and I continued our walks. The curlews had been heard again and I took her to see them. I showed her the spaces in the rocks where, come spring, we would collect seabird eggs once again. She was wearing lipstick, an orange colour like the underside of a crab. It made her teeth look quite yellow, and was smudged on the left side.

'I like your lipstick,' I said to her as we were walking back.

'Oh, thank you,' she said, as though she was surprised to be still wearing it. 'I wear it all the time at home. It feels strange to wear it here but . . . but I suppose I'm just used to it.'

'Do all the women wear lipstick in England?'

'Not all, no. Many do. At the university it is a little frowned upon. But in the towns, at dances . . . it's everyone.'

We watch a shower of gannets fall from the cliffs into the water. I tell her a story about them from the previous year. The level of the sea had changed and the birds had not realised. They dived with such force that most of them snapped their necks. We were fishing them from the water for months.

'I'll have to put that in the book,' she said. I felt very good about that.

The clouds at the edge of the water had begun to turn a dark grey. The boats were on the main stretch of water below the cliffs, coming in.

'I think there is a storm coming,' I said. 'We should head back.'

She looked out. 'How do you know? The water is still.'

I heard a curlew wheel in the grass behind us.

'Some of the older generations believe the curlews cry when a storm is coming. It's an omen that someone will die at sea.'

Joan studied the grass.

'Probably a change in air pressure makes them call. A change in their territory. Wouldn't you say?'

I didn't reply. Often my conversations with Joan went that way: me telling her something she did not know before, her arguing with it.

~

When we reached her lodging, she asked me to wait outside a moment. I felt the first drops of rain fall around me, watched them form small craters in the sandy ground. She opened the door a crack and pressed something wrapped in paper out of it.

'I appreciate our walks,' she said.

I thanked her.

Her hand replied in the gap, waving me away.

I unwrapped it as I walked. A lipstick in a royal blue

casing, with gold lines around the lid. I came home and put it on my lips. It was the orange-crab colour. I looked in the mirror. I liked the way I looked. I turned and put some on Llinos. I had to look away. She looked just like our mother.

The wind roared around the chapel on Sunday. It was filled with the smell of wet wool. Shining with water that had dripped from the roof. Joan was at the altar, answering questions about the project.

'We believe there is great wisdom, in people who live with the land. In ordinary, working folk. We live in difficult times, as you all know. Difficult economically, socially. We believe that a return to the land is needed, a return to a certain way of life. It might sound strange to you, but really we want to preserve the things you know.'

Joan's face was redder than I'd ever seen it, struggling with the cold or the pressure of speaking.

Edward looked at me, and raised his eyebrows. His reaction made me smile. He stood up, touched Joan on the shoulder. Joan jumped, nervous, and sat down.

'We want to record your songs, your stories. Nothing more.'

'Preserve a sense of true Britishness,' Joan added. She gestured wildly. 'The island. The island!'

'We're grateful for your cooperation.'

I heard a voice behind me. Marc, a herring fisherman in the pew behind us, leaning over to my father.

'Is that the Englishman? Is that him?' the voice said.

'Listen. This day, didn't I see a *toili* coming down from the cliffs.'

The woman sitting in front of me turned and shushed them.

'Didn't I see it,' Marc continued. 'On the hills it was. Dropped down and I stepped aside to let it pass but of course it never did come round the bend.'

'We don't have *toili* on the island,' Tad replied, barely turning his head. 'That's mainland folk. Mainland superstition.'

'I'm telling you what I saw. All men dressed in black, I saw it. Grey faces, no features. No feet, their legs going on to nothing. Walking along the hills. White flowers all in the grass suddenly.'

The woman in front of them shook her head, like she was trying to rid a fly from her ear.

'Is there something you wish to add?'

Reverend Jones looked towards us. I felt my cheeks redden. Tad rose from his seat.

'Carry on, Reverend,' Tad said. 'My apologies.'

'Marc says he saw a *toili* when the English feller arrived,' the woman in front of us said. She had a white bonnet on her head, rimy yellow where it met her skin.

Reverend Jones sighed.

'As we've been saying, the English feller and *woman* have names.'

Reverend Jones was higher than Edward, on the raised altar platform. He placed a hand on Edward's shoulder.

'And there won't be talk of toilies in the house of God.'

I looked at Joan, compelled to apologise. She was writing everything down in her little book, her face bright with pride.

A storm arrived. Black clouds, the birds deafening and then silent. Rooms full of new shadow. Spiders seeking refuge inside the house. In the mornings, Llinos and I sat on the floor at the end of our bed, and prayed with our hands flat on the mattress. Tad went out with the other men to help man the lighthouse, in his long rubber boots. How I hated those boots, which would drag him underwater if he was swept away. He returned red-faced, his hands bleeding. I soaked them in water and tied his bootlaces for him. The wind closed in around the house.

Overnight, the waves took two sheep that had wandered from shelter. Some of the boats did not come back, and women filed inside the lighthouse to listen to the coastguard on the wireless. Their breath steamed up the windows.

Llinos kept a line of pine cones on her windowsill and studied them in the mornings. I'd watch her sit next to Elis on the floor. She peeled away their outer layers, and announced to Elis that it would be a dry day, or found them hard and shut, and said it would rain. Sometimes they went hard and their spines split in two, in which case she lifted up Elis's ear gently, whispered that she wasn't sure, and put it back down again.

The windows were lined with fog in the morning, and

I drew shapes on them: fish, seals, and small faces. If the rain was hard, I was stuck inside. I would run outside to fill pots with earth, and plant beans inside them. I had a thought we might need them for spring. When they grew white shoots, I was reminded suddenly of Mam's days lying in the dark of her room, curled up and pale.

As winter comes, the islanders continue to fish in treacherous conditions. We hear from our host that a young mainland fisherman had gone missing over the side of a stout crabber one week previous. The island fishermen remembered seeing the boat, its red sails and painted deckhouse, on the water.

The young man's body is found in one of the coves of the island, ahead of a stormy night. He is identified by a birthmark on his shoulder. As no boats are going out, and the body is in a state of half-rot, the man will be buried on the island. The cemetery is full of such graves.

SJCEG Disc 7.

You're a man from a faraway land,
We'll bury you with our own dead,
We'll bury you with our own priest.
You can call our land your home,
When our dead return, you'll return with them.

*Collected 2.11.38 from W. Rhys (b. 1901), of Y Ty Bryn
(The Hill House). Folk song.*

A lamb was lost on the moor behind the cliffs. All night we were looking for her, the rain lashing at us in sheets, the wind almost blowing us from the cliffs in the dark. Merionn with the mother on a rope so the lamb could follow her voice, all of us following using our last oil in the oil lamps. One of the women on the hill turned to me, said, A few of us have been having dreams. About the whale, and about a woman coming out of the water. Have you been having dreams like that? It doesn't seem a good sign, the woman said.

Another sidled up next to me. We wondered about Lukasz, in the lighthouse. Why he didn't warn us. Perhaps because he wasn't born here.

They began to talk about Olwen, and I strained to listen. The sea was heavy, and the sound was hurting my ears. Her baby had died a little after dawn, just before the storm began. It had been too late to fetch a doctor. Despite the rain, the husband had gone to the lighthouse, and sent a message over radio telegraph to the coastguard. The coastguard telephoned the mainland, who granted permission for the child to be buried without an inquest. There would be a mound of earth behind the chapel to mark it, covered with a ring of shells.

The lamb was found nestled in tree roots, shivering. Dai's wife carried the lamb home like a baby. Some said it slept in their bed, that they kept a paraffin lamp on in the stable. For days afterwards our clothes were haired with white wool, curls of it, from where we had pushed between the bodies of the sheep.

~

One of the women had turned to me, asked about Edward and Joan. She said Joan had turned up to her house one day, watched the woman make butter. She had said some strange things, about protecting the land. I gave her a pat of butter, the woman said, and told her she can come back and make it any time she likes.

The women around us laughed at that.

Edward turned up at the house, soaking wet. I let him inside, sat him by the fire. He wanted to see my embroidery, he said.

I brought them out. I showed him the ones I was most proud of: a Christmas feast, everyone eating at a long table. A large fish on a plate, into which I had sewn small beads. Water, with small white boats.

I showed him one I was working on, bigger than usual. I had sewed a structure of a chapel. At ground-level, next to it, a funeral was taking place. Everyone in black, with white flowers growing on the ground around them. Beneath them, the coffin as it was lowered, and skeletons. The skeletons walked along the bottom of the material, from where they floated up through the chapel, out through the roof, and became grey gulls.

'I thought I might place it on a quilt,' I said.

'A little morbid, don't you think?'

He took them back with him. Joan wanted to see them, and they wanted to write some notes about them for the book. He hadn't brought his camera, he said, because of the rain.

SJCEG Disc 11.

Once there was a mother who lived on the island, who had three daughters. The daughters were each very lovely: one was beautiful, one was kind, one was supremely intelligent. The sea grew jealous of the daughters and so sent each of them mad, so that they would dive into the water when walking on the cliffs. The woman waited for the sea to return her daughters. She prayed to it every day. But the sea could only return them as whales, who would sometimes come up to the surface of the water, only to be taken away again.

Collected 7.11.38 from R. Moore (Crabber, b. 1895), of Y Bwthyn Pren (The Wooden Cottage). Folktale variation.

As soon as the storm arrived, it left. I woke and my room was washed with cold light. Leah's goats had been let out of their shelter, and I could hear them calling to each other.

In the outbuilding, Merionn clutched his hat to his chest as he spoke, a long story about a woman on a cliff being swallowed up by a sea-snake and transformed into a sea storm. I could tell he was nervous, that the hat was to stop his hand from shaking. Edward furrowed his brow. He tugged the elbow of my dress.

'Can you ask him to put that away? And then ask him to start from the top.'

Merionn did not speak English, so I translated the request and he nodded. I wrote out the English translation of the story, and Joan read it carefully. I watched a bird in the roof of the building fly from one side to the other. I could wear one of my better dresses now the storm was over. It was dark blue, with boning up the side which stuck into my hip, and made me sit up straight. Joan looked over to me and passed my translation back. I instinctively smoothed my hair down. When Merionn finished, Edward asked him to state his name and occupation.

'Merionn Davies. Ffermer Dafydd.'

'Sheep farmer,' I said.

'Ask him – do you have any sources for this?'

'What do you mean?'

'Does this come from anywhere? Probably not, but ask. Might be from music, a named musician, anything like that?'

'Granda played the harp,' Merionn said.

'No, I mean—' Edward shook his head. He wrote something down.

Merionn left before we were finished, said he could smell water on the air and needed to get his sheep in shelter.

I asked Joan if it was a problem, that Merionn didn't know who had written the song. Joan shook her head emphatically. She said it was exactly what they were looking for.

My grandfather had been a whaler, I told the microphone. Edward had asked me to test it, but when I began speaking he asked me to carry on.

The ship was called the *Diana*.

We have a photograph of my grandfather, although we don't know who took it. He is at the bow of the ship, looking out to sea. You can't see the entire ship but it looks big. My grandfather is leaning against a rope. The landscape behind him has a lot of ice, white hills. Behind him in the water is a dark shape, moving the water up to a ridge.

On that trip he went up to Greenland. He got iced in for so long that when he got back home he walked in and frightened my great-grandmother who had given up hope for his safe return, and took him for a stranger. More than a stranger, she thought he was a ghost, and threw salt at him.

Collected 10.11.38 from Y M Llan (b. 1920), of Bwthyn Rhosyn (Rose Cottage). Family history.

~

I watched Edward write out a label for the disc as I spoke.

'What do you make of Joan?' Edward asked me afterwards, while I sat transcribing my own voice.

He gave me a scone to eat, and the currants were hard

and chewy. Next to me, Edward drew out a view of the island from the window next to us. I watched as faraway houses appeared, figures and fishing nets and sheep. A chapel in the foreground, dry-stone walls laden with moss. He shaded in the sky, the dark clouds of winter. Long hill-sides of clean grass.

'I think she's very nice,' I said.

He looked over his shoulder. I noticed a window in the drawing, a woman standing and looking out.

'Did you know she is one of Mosley's?' he said.

'One of what?'

He told me everything. A political movement on the mainland; how proudly Joan had told him about the rallies she attended, about protests in the street. That her mother had been a Suffragette, that Joan had gone to Oxford, and now she wouldn't listen to anyone telling her she was wrong.

'Filled her head with fancy notions.'

'What kind of notions?'

'Well. Fascism, Manod. Dangerous ideas.'

'Do you believe in it?'

'No, no. I don't consider myself very political.'

He drew a stretch of dark sea behind the island. Small houses on the other side, on the mainland.

He tore the page from his sketchbook, and handed it to me.

'You can keep this,' he said.

~

At home, I pinned the drawing to the wall on my side of the bed. Llinos chided me, saying that it would fall on us while we slept. I felt sharply conscious of Edward lying in a bed not far from me, the same images of the island in his thoughts. I felt as though I could see into the future, how I might remember the island after leaving, its nettle-flanked paths and crowds of birds.

Llinos began to snore in her sleep, splaying her arms out over my chest. I hissed at her to move over. Birds outside were crying, finding their burrows in the night. I traced my fingers over each part of the drawing, finding the woman in the window.

Finally the wind cleared, and we were able to make passage to the mainland. Tad took the rusted boat. The sea looked filthy and grey, and was covered in a horrible yellow foam.

I stood where there were women sorting through that morning's catch, loading it into the boats to sell. One of them was sat on a stool, gutting rockfish, flinging them into a low tray in front of her. Pink liquid was oozing between the tray's wooden slats, the pool getting bigger. Her hands worked quickly, effortlessly. The woman dropped her gutting knife, and I bent down to pick it up. She crouched at the same time, her foot knocking against the knife's handle, and the tool span towards my hand. I felt a sharp pain, and when I turned my hand over I saw a small cut, bright red. The woman tutted.

'You should be more careful,' a voice said above my head. Edward.

'It was an accident.'

He took a handkerchief from his pocket and pressed it to my hand. It had already stopped bleeding, but I let him keep his hand there. My hand throbbed against his. When he took the material away the salt air set in, stinging up to my elbow.

'I would have thought you were used to hand injuries.'

'Sorry?'

'Your embroidery. Joan loved it. She wondered if you could write some short labels for it.'

'Of course,' I said. We stood in silence a while. I saw Tad, down at the water's edge, notice us talking. He put his cages down and headed towards us.

'You've grown a beard,' I said to Edward.

'That's me. Robinson Crusoe.'

He turned to leave, lifting his hat. He placed his hand on my back as he moved past me. Tad reached me soon after, his face wide and expectant.

'It's work,' I told him.

Tad shook his head. He turned back, distracted, and knocked into the gutting woman. Rockfish went spilling over the sand, each fish writhing for air. The woman threw herself onto the ground to catch them. The women around us laughed at her. I tried to help the woman gather them up, but she pushed my hands away.

The last time I saw my mother was when we sat at the table in the kitchen and prepared a bowl of mussels. It was rare for Mam to leave her bed at that point, and she came into the kitchen slowly, as though she was growing out from the wall. We worked silently. I was careless with the knife and nicked my finger at the join. Mam took my hand and placed it in her mouth, until the bleeding stopped. When I close my eyes and try to picture her face, I only see a pair of mussel shells, slowly opening in my hands.

Puffins gathered on the edge of the cliffs, finally leaving for winter. I thought they looked ridiculous when they walked, like tiny people on two legs. They reminded me of the old generation's stories: fairies on the side of the road, stealing coins.

Leah brought round a dress for me to sew. It was November and Mari Lwyd was only a few weeks away, she said. The dress was green wool, with a dark check pattern, and the bottom half was riddled with moth-eaten holes. Could I fix it? I told her I could. She asked me to come round to help her process a bag of wool into yarn. I told her that I would come in the next few days.

I sewed small brown flowers over the holes in the dress. Against the green they did not stand out too much, and you only saw them if you looked closely.

Elis sat by the door, waiting for Tad, watching any shadows that passed underneath it. I called him, tried to get him to run over to me, but he ignored me.

I turned the dress over, to start the other side, when I was distracted by a commotion in front of the house. I heard voices and running feet. I got up as Llinos threw the door open and shut it. I put my face to the window. Two boys, Cadoc and Tomos, backed off like spooked cats.

'What was that?'

'Nothing,' Llinos said. 'Just chasing.'

~

I found her crying in the kitchen, later. Long, wailing sobs. I pulled her into my stomach. One of her skeleton models was laid out in front of her, and in her hand was a broken bone. Llinos cried like a baby, red-faced and choking. The bone was the size and shape of a needle.

'I broke it,' she said. 'It felt strange and I broke it.'

When she calmed down, we glued the skeleton together, replacing the broken bone. The needle shone silver. I only had one. Leah's dress would have to wait.

I spent all night writing out the descriptions of my embroideries for Edward and Joan. I had to describe what each one depicted, and how I had acquired the thread. Joan and Edward were photographing them along with other things: a quilt Leah had made over ten years, a jacket from a fisherman who claimed it had been passed through his family for two centuries. The jacket stank, and looked like an old rag.

Once I had finished writing, I had to submerge the label in water, and then paste it to the back of each embroidery. Edward had given me a kind of special paper. Once it had dried, it would stick in place.

I repeated the process for every embroidery. By the time I was finished, my hands ached and the skin around my nails was coming away. I peeled them until the skin looked red and unhealthy, wiped them on my dress, and went to bed.

Joan and Edward were already inside the chapel when I arrived, reading from a stack of letters. I had brought my embroideries in a leather suitcase. Joan was wearing a silk scarf over her hair, a pattern in bright red and green. As I placed my embroideries in a neat stack on the table, I saw an official-looking letter with the words NATIONAL SALVAGE COUNCIL stamped over it.

'Are those your friends, Joan?' I said, gesturing at the letter. 'The ones you spoke about at dinner?'

Joan peered down at it over her glasses.

'Yes, they should arrive in the next few days. I told them to come quickly.'

'Will they really take the whale?'

'They'll take as much of it as they can.'

Edward laughed suddenly.

'What's that?'

'Listen to this – it's a letter someone sent to the paper, but it was returned here.'

'I am 18 years old, and in want of a wife. I have hair, teeth, am a Baptist. I have a bull, two heifers, and five white geese – wait for it, wait – I am an excellent forager of seaweed, sea lettuce, and limpets in the winter.'

'What a Casanova!'

'It's because we don't go fishing in the winter. There's

no herring or lobster. Also, you might have noticed that it's dangerous to go out at the moment.'

'No, no. We know.' They exchanged glances. 'It's just—'

'Funny,' Edward said. 'It's just amusing.'

'I thought you liked our food.'

'We do, we do, we're joking around, Manod. It's more that it's . . . old-fashioned, in the way that it's written.'

I wanted to ask why, but could not find the words. I did not like their tone. Edward sucked air in through his nostrils, smiled and shook his head. Joan's shoulders trembled, as though holding in a cough.

'Who is it?' I asked. 'Who is the writer?'

I did not need to ask: the only eighteen-year-old boy on the island was Llew.

I asked for the day off: Tad needed help drying out fish for winter, and Llinos help with her schoolwork. They said yes.

~

The schoolchildren were enamoured with the whale, and Llinos was supposed to make a picture of it. She decided to make a mask. I had a small set of paints that Rosslyn had given me and we mixed a close approximation of the colours. I drew out the shape for her, and the features. I liked drawing the eyes, with their cobweb of wrinkles. When we were finished, we had painted it altogether too blue. The whale was really a kind of dark grey, like a stone. I didn't say anything to Llinos, and she seemed happy with it. She took it and ran to show her friend Tomos. I could hear her pant with excitement as she ran down the path.

I went to the dock, and watched the women haul in the fish. They were working overtime after the storm. On one side I saw Olwen, staring at her hands. I thought about going to the mainland, and tried to calculate how long it would take me to get somewhere else, Paris or London, and then how much it would cost. I heard the women talk about planting corn in a field near the sea-edge. A cat came near my feet, drawn by the smell. It jumped into my lap and I let it stay there, its flank wet against my chest.

Edward came to see me in the evening. He was worried they had offended me. I told him they hadn't.

'I wouldn't like you to think I have a poor opinion of you, Manod,' he said.

'I don't,' I said.

'Do you know what I'm getting at?'

He came close to me, close to my face, and then pulled away.

'I like the white dress you wear,' he said, as he walked away. 'I like it very much.'

~

There was rain and I lay awake listening to it. Heavy rain, coming down in sheets. The sound of it gurgling in the drain in the yard, dripping from the roof. The sound of it reminded me of when Rosslyn was still on the island, and she and I would go down to the coves to draw. Rosslyn had a small set of paints she got one Christmas, and we would look in the rock pools and paint what was there. Scarlet anemones, all the greens and reds and darks of the algae and weeds. We would sit so still and for so long the water would begin to make noises at us. Small creatures would lip the edge of the water with a popping or slopping sound, or release a stream of bubbles. I fell asleep thinking about it, and when I woke my pillow was cold and slightly damp.

I saw Edward every night for the next week, waiting until Llinos was asleep and then slipping from our bed.

The sheep on the hillside watched me as I walked over to the chapel. I thought I saw a light inside one of the houses, a figure come to the window. There was no one there. The sea whispered, let me walk in quiet. I thought of a story my mother told me, about the sea turning to stone.

~

Edward's body was pale and noduled, like the body of an insect. We met in the chapel outbuilding, because he and Joan slept in the same room. He laid a wool blanket on the floor for us, and two striped pillows. The place was lit by moonlight, our skin a sour grey. Edward had muscles, but they were tight and lean, and his belly was rounded and striped down the centre with dark hair. I tried not to think about the way I looked: my dirty, dry heels and wiry limbs.

~

'You would love the mainland,' he said, afterwards, leaning up on his elbows. 'I think you would really thrive there.'

This was a conversation we often had. He would tell me about his life there. His small apartment in a terraced house, with a landlady who grew yellow roses. His friends, who were mostly artists, and his brother, another scholar. Most nights I asked him to describe the things he ate there: ice-cream, roast beef, sweet breads.

'I could come with you,' I said. 'You and Joan.'

'I have a friend,' he said, 'in Paris. He makes records. I thought I would play our recordings for him.'

'I thought I'd go to university.'

'You could do anything.'

He turned and kissed me, running his fingers gently down my shoulder.

~

He showed me the darkroom that he had fashioned at the side of the chapel. There was a heavy sheet of canvas we had to walk through.

Inside, the photographs he was developing were hanging on a line in a small alcove. I saw a photograph of one of my embroideries, and one of a group of islanders I recognised. I read the back of it. Written in pencil: *An island family enjoys a picnic.* No one in the photograph was related. And we never ate outside. A photograph of Cadoc: *A young island boy, training to be a sheep farmer, or fisherman of whale shark.* Cadoc's family kept cattle. I had never heard of a whale shark.

Edward beckoned me further into the darkroom, to show me a series of photographs he had taken on the mainland. There had been a whale washed up somewhere there too. The whale was lying on a platform on the back half of a lorry, with wires holding its head upright and mouth open. Its eye looked right out at you, and though it was small, it caught the light like a marble. There was a crowd around it, a man on the left-hand side laughing, another lighting a cigarette. Lots of hats. A woman held her small child above her head. On the platform was a young woman in a pale swimsuit and a pearl necklace, holding up a sign, and a handsome man pointing to a harpoon at his feet. The whale's mouth had long fringes inside, like silk.

In the other photographs, the position of the crowd and the signs of the young lady changed: dorsal fin, baleen, upper jaw, lower jaw. The final photograph showed a trailer behind the lorry. GOLIATH, THE GREAT WHALE was painted along the side.

'I was quite disappointed by it,' Edward said, behind me. 'The whale. I thought it would be blue. Really it was a horrible sort of dour grey.'

He put his hands over my hips as I ran my fingers over the pictures. He moved them over my belly, down between my legs. I thought to protest, but gave in soon enough. It felt good to be desired by somebody like him.

~

He fell asleep quickly, and I heard his breathing slow beside his dreaming. I thought about the whale that had washed up here, and the one in the photographs, wondered if they had ever seen each other. I imagined them swimming together, around the continents Sister Mary had told us about at school, leading one another through the tunnels of the sea.

SJCEG Disc 16.

When my father was a child, he says, there was another island attached to this one. My father would run over there with his friends and play. It was a very small thing, room enough for ten or so people to stand on it, and only appeared at low tide. He has many memories of it, of him and the other children watching the diving birds come up with fish, sometimes seeing octopus on the seabed. You can't see that island anymore. Tad said something in the water had swallowed it up.

Like an evil spirit?

Oh yes, and my Mam said it too.

Does she believe in evil spirits?

She says there is a spirit that overturns fishing boats and empties lobster pots. And some people do say that a boat can be touched by the devil and then has to be blessed by a priest with holy water before she can go out again–

We don't have a priest, we have a minister.

This is the truth I'm telling you. Once my father spoke to a woman on the mainland, who said she was born there. They were in a pub by the docks. He was listening to her and then suddenly she was gone. He asked around but no one knew her. No one had even seen her with their eyes.

It's difficult to believe.

It must be believed. You have to believe it, you see. Why lie? You have to believe it.

Collected 17.11.38 from M. Brith (b. 1919), residing Pen Craig (Rock Top). Additional voice of M. Llan. Family story.

When I returned home in the morning, there was a letter waiting on the step. I recognised the handwriting, the blue fountain-pen ink. It was from Llew. His mother must have received it, and brought it round. I opened it outside, leaning against the door. Apparently his mother had written to him about the English researchers.

I have thought of you often on the mainland. The factory is not as easy as I expected. There are jobs, but too many people who need them. We queue outside the factory each morning and hope to be given a shift. Me and the other men. One of them sings, collects money that way. He reminds me of you.

Did you find work with the English visitors? What are they like? My Mam says they are very polite, but odd, and the man has smooth hands like a child. How is Llinos?

I do miss the island. Do you remember in spring, the well outside my house would spawn with shrimp? I would always show you them, their stumpy, half-growing limbs. When we collected water we had to pick them out. You would always drink your tea with your teeth together, to form a kind of sieve against them, in case there were any we missed. I feel very fond about those times.

I'm writing to tell you I've decided to join up. Finding work is too hard and I can't face living on the island. It seems there will be a war soon. When I enlisted they took a photograph of me, and gave me chocolate, a compass and a Stanley knife. I've enclosed my army photograph, and a spare compass I was given. I thought you might like them. I worked out that my barracks are exactly east of Rose Cottage.

If you want to write back, you can write to the address on the back of the envelope.

Then, written quickly, in pencil rather than pen. *Please write back.*

The photograph of Llew was beautiful. His skin was clear and his hair very neat. He wasn't smiling. I took the compass out and watched the needle shudder.

I began to wear my clothes differently, and look at them in new ways. I planned the outfit I would wear to sing for Edward's friend in Paris. I separated out my good clothes, any that were silk or velvet. I wore the same tunic most days, which was scratchy and bunched around my waist. I wanted the rest to be clean in my suitcase, for when I arrived on the mainland. In my head, I set aside skirts and blouses for Llinos to wear as she grew.

In the morning Joan knocked on our cottage door. She had Edward's camera; and wanted to take photographs of the inside of the house. I wasn't expecting her, and hadn't tidied it. She insisted she had warned me before the storm set in.

While she took photographs of the front door and yard, I hid our old plates and dirty clothes wherever I could. In cupboards, under the bed. I threw the stained tablecloth straight out of the window, leaving the gleaming wood beneath on show. I still had on my nightdress, and I quickly changed into a dress I wore the day before, which I had folded on the back of a chair.

Joan was silent, and I trailed her like a shadow. I tried to see the house as she would. Our jars and cans of food, made to last a winter. The dried herbs hanging from hooks. Old blankets, quilts. Llinos's chapel shoes, scuffed and abandoned by the door.

'You don't need to follow me around,' Joan said. 'It's almost impolite.'

'I'm sorry. Is it? Impolite?'

She smiled curtly, and left the room. I heard her sigh, and the click of the camera.

While she was busy, I laid out a scenescape on the table. I retrieved a column of lace we never used, and laid it as a tablecloth. A brass candlestick, two new candles. The sugar bowl. A spoon I rubbed against my dress until it shone. When Joan appeared again, I showed the result to her.

'You try too hard to impress us, Manod,' she said.

We were making Christmas cake. Llinos was sifting through dried fruit, picking out any hard bits of stalk. I weighed sugar. The delicate grains kept dropping onto the table. Llinos picked them up by pressing them with her finger, and flicking them back into the bowl. She was absorbed in it. I thought I could watch her for a long time.

She only nodded when I told her I would be going to the mainland after all, with Joan and Edward. She asked me when, I said I was not sure. Possibly in the spring, after Christmas had passed. She carried on dabbing up the sugar with her finger, holding the grains up to the light.

'I saw Edward in the yard,' Llinos said. 'A few times. Taking pictures of the house.'

He had not mentioned that to me. We slipped butter into the bowl in silence. There was a cry in the yard.

'It's a little owl,' Llinos said, without looking up.

I went to the window, which had steamed up. I felt Llinos's body behind me.

'It's lucky,' she said. 'It's good luck.'

A few days passed. I did not hear from Joan or Edward. I went by the chapel and found the doors locked. I would knock on the door and, while I was waiting for an answer, study the chapel notices, the mosses growing behind the glass. Eventually I returned home.

Reverend Jones said they were going down to the shore each day. From the hill I could see the sand was pocked with footprints. On the day I finally saw them, a group of children came running from one end of the beach, chased by Edward. They were shrieking, playing. I knew the children were scared of Edward's camera, because Llinos had told me. She didn't like it either; she said it looked like a cat's pupil.

When I reached the shore, Edward was sat with the children. They were teaching him the Welsh words for animals, for cat, dog, sheep, bird, mouse. One of them pulled on his sleeve and yelled other words for illnesses, for flu, cough, fever.

He turned and saw me before I reached them. I waved. He nodded, and turned back to the children. What is the word for pig? he said to them, scratching his chin. For big pig? For ugly? His voice became lost in the children's laughter.

'How are you?' I asked his shoulder.

'How do I say, go away?'

The children collapsed around him in laughter.

'I'm only joking, Manod,' he said, turning briefly to meet my gaze. 'But I am getting a few things here. Could we speak another time?'

I nodded. He did not wait for me to answer.

~

In the evenings I tried to focus on my sewing. I missed my embroideries, and wondered when Edward and Joan would return them. My fingers felt restless.

I thought of my mother's prayer cushion, and drew out a ring of trees with the thread. Black branches, thin, like hairs. I tried to sew birds, but the colours seemed too garish. I tried to draw a weasel, which Joan had described on her family's estate, but as I had never seen one it too looked strange, outsized, like a snake with tiny legs. Frustrated, I dropped the hoop onto the floor, making Elis jump. There was so much of the world I had not seen.

One of Tad's newspapers was on the chair next to me. I picked it up. A picture of stern, dark men marching in a line, and a ring made by his tea-cup. I read the words Edward had said – Fascists, Black-shirts. I thought of Joan chastising me. Elis jumped onto my lap, and put his jaw against my neck. I felt his heartbeat against my shoulder, his limbs finding a comfortable place to rest.

SJCEG Disc 19.

It was a story I heard from a sailor in Scotland, not anyone from around here. But my children, and my nieces and nephews, they love it. I suppose they will tell it to their children. Because I tell it to them. It starts in lots of different ways. Sometimes I say it is about their mothers or older sisters and brothers, or that it happens at Christmas. But the basic story stays the same. A man sees a circle of fairies dancing on a beach one evening at dusk. When the fairies notice him, they quickly pull on sealskins and run into the water. One fairy is left behind, running here and there as though looking for something. The man finds her sealskin before she does, and throws it into the long dune grass.

The man persuades the fairy girl to marry him, and she bears him children. He always finds her trying to speak to the seals on the beach, or find her sealskin, but eventually she gives up. One year – and sometimes it's a long winter killing away the grass, sometimes a hot summer doing the same, sometimes children playing hide-and-seek on the beach – the sealskin is found in the sand by her children, and they bring it home to her, thinking they want to keep it.

Without a beat, their mother takes the skin and disappears. Her husband finds her on the beach shedding her clothes into a crumpled heap and stepping into the old skin. She dives into the water, never to be seen again. What happens to the children? I never get that far.

Collected 28.11.38 from P. Howell (Retired Lighthouse Keeper b. 1850), of Y Tyddyn Bach (Little Farm). Folktale variation.

I found Joan and Edward on the beach, taking photographs of a fisherman in the water. They had positioned him near the beach, in the shallow water at the base of the cliffs. Normally fishermen wouldn't dare go into that part of the sea around the island: currents gathered there that could throw you against the rocks. The man in the water was John. He had black hair, black eyes, and a black beard. Once he had shown me a tattoo he got at sea, of a mermaid, which swam up the back of his leg. His clothes were soaked through, and he was standing against the waves as they crashed around his hips.

'Could you lunge?' shouted Joan, from the beach. 'As though you are catching it with your bare hands?'

I asked Edward what they were doing.

'We wanted to get some action photographs. Showing the fishermen, how they fish. But I didn't want to get in a boat with the camera, in case it got wet. So we're just getting an example of it here.'

'But that isn't how we fish.'

'I know that, Manod. We'll describe how you fish, the picture is just an illustration. We'll write something in the caption—'

'I can help you write it.'

Something passed over his face. A thought I couldn't read.

'Of course,' he said.

Joan was calling him over. She turned and noticed I was there, beckoned me over, too.

'Manod,' she said, putting her fingers on the bridge of her nose. 'Can you explain to him what we want? I just want him to pull up one of the cages with his hands, and hold it up for the camera.'

Poor John looked miserable as a wave went crashing over his shoulders. Foam spread on the surface of the water around his body. I wondered what they had promised him. I called out to him, explained to him in Welsh what he was supposed to do. He shrugged at me. I asked him what they were paying him. He said they weren't. I said I would give him a few coins.

Eventually, John turned sideways and thrust his hands into the water. He ducked down and disappeared below an oncoming wave. I held my breath. Joan muttered something, quietly. Edward moved forward with the camera. When John emerged, the lobster cage in his hands, he threw it high above his head. I heard the camera's shutter going off, Joan yelling *Hold it! Hold it!* Water ran from John's chest until another wave took him, knocked him off his feet. I wondered if, in all the commotion, the lobster managed to get away.

~

Joan entered the outbuilding first, shaking her headscarf free of water. I shut the door behind us.

'I got soaked,' Joan said, gruffly.

Her hair was dark at the hairline. She sat at the table, and I sat across from her. She passed me paper and a pen so I could start transcribing. She placed her gold-rimmed glasses on her nose, and made notes on the back of some of Edward's photographs. Normally we talked for a while before starting work.

'I do envy you, Manod, living here,' she said, without looking up.

She picked up another photograph, and studied it.

'There are few places left like this. I'm not sure you appreciate it.'

She turned back to her writing. I picked at my fingers, found a loose nail. I tried to understand her change in mood. Joan glanced up at me, when she realised I was still watching her.

'Why did you ask John to go into the water?' I asked.

'What do you mean?'

'It was very rough today.'

'He's a fisherman.'

'We don't learn to swim, not properly. I told you that. The sea is too dangerous, there is no point—'

'Well, he didn't come to any harm, did he?'

'He could have.'

Joan finished her notes, scribbling hard. She dotted the end of a sentence with a violent jab.

'If there is something you'd like to say, Manod, you can say it.'

'I think it was dangerous. And you only did it for selfish reasons, to make your book more exciting.'

'I think you are naive. I think you are too young and too sheltered here, and don't know how the world works.'

Her voice was sharp. She sighed, took her glasses off. I ripped the hangnail, and felt an orb of blood forming at the edge of my thumb.

'I may as well come out with it. I have seen lipstick on some of Edward's clothes. Coral-coloured, the one I gave to you.'

I said nothing.

'You should be careful, Manod. Chasing men that way.'

'I don't see how it's your business.'

'Bedding your *employer*. We gave you an opportunity. You've squandered it.'

I felt shame on me, hot and stinging.

'Edward says you are a Fascist,' I said. 'Is that true?'

We watched each other for a moment.

'I have been reading about them in the paper.'

'And I suppose you agree with Edward, that it's all sorts of nonsense.'

'It's hard to know how the world works,' I said. 'When you're so far away from it here.'

Joan rubbed her hands over her face. I was surprised to see her eyes tearing up. Her eyelashes were thin and dark. I realised she looked older than when she arrived, that the weather had given her skin dry patches all over.

'Yes,' she said. 'Of course. I suppose I'm angry at Edward more than anything.'

She looked at my hands but did not reach for them. She picked up her pen, fiddled with it. It splashed black ink onto her blouse.

'I just want the book to be perfect,' she said. 'If we can't capture a sense of the island, then there's . . .'

She trailed off.

'The island that's in your head. I don't think it exists,' I said.

She looked up at me, her fountain pen pressed a dark circle of ink on the page. I thought I saw anger flash across her features.

'Go home, Manod,' she said, quietly, without looking me in the eye. 'You're dismissed.'

'I am home,' I said blankly back.

Outside, a trail of children wove their way towards the beach. One of them had made a mask of the whale out of paper, with a flap for its toothed grin.

I helped Llinos bathe. Her face was pink and round like a moon. I asked her if Cadoc was still bothering her, and she didn't answer. She covered herself with her hands.

'Don't look at me, please,' she said.

I scrubbed myself with the brush for a long time when it was my turn in the water, until I was covered in red welts over my arms, torso, neck. Then I held my breath and ducked my head under the water. Strange ringing in my ears. I imagined myself coming apart into a jelly pink mass, and then coming back together again. I imagined I was a whale, and I disappeared beneath the ground.

In the orange glow of the oil lamp, Leah moved wool from the sack between her feet to her wooden paddles. She brushed it through, creating long strands of wool which I took and thinned out into yarn.

Her radio began to stammer, and she asked me to turn it off. She sat still, and said she was thinking of selling her land.

'Why?'

'Why does anyone?'

'Do you need money?'

'Dafydd wants to move. His brother on the mainland has offered part of his farm. Says we can take the goats by boat, and someone would have Meg from us, probably Merionn.'

She sighed.

'The roof is falling to pieces.'

As though on cue, the roof released a long dribble of water. It ran across the alcove, where it had already discoloured the wallpaper to an ominous yellow.

I asked Leah if she had seen the English couple. Joan had not spoken to me since the day at the outbuilding. She and Edward left translations for me on the table. I had seen her at her window and waved, and she had turned around.

'I need a doctor,' Leah muttered. 'My fingers . . .'

I looked up at her, as she rubbed her hands, her eyes closed in pain. I thought they had looked swollen. The wool in my hands felt clammy, and I stretched my fingers beneath it. Her sheepdog, Meg, sidled up to us, smelling of rot, pushing her wet snout against my ankle.

~

That evening, the house was asleep and I padded to my and Llinos's room. I finished a translation of a song, writing slowly so that Llinos wasn't woken by the sound of my scratching the page. The song was about a boat reaching the lighthouse to service it in a storm. Notes extended to mimic the waves. A shout above cruel wind – the fog horn, the yelling of the men. In the final verse, the men try to return to the mainland, and drown. A horse waits on the harbour wall.

On the back of the paper were some of Joan's notes. I hadn't realised I'd taken them with my translation. I read them idly.

Every islander contains a seed of wisdom, an affinity with the land. It is as though the water of the body has spilled out of them to create the sea, so familiar are they with it. Sea widows, childless mothers, all wear their sorrow in their black clothing, their salt-worn skin. The sea is their taunting lover, and yet the sea is worshipped, in embroideries, in heirloom fishing tools, boots and jackets—

I read it over and over. My chest cramped. Who was she talking about? I did not know these people. I ripped the paper up and threw it onto the fire. I curled up into a ball, put the blanket over my head. Under the wool, my tears were oily, and tasted of sweat.

~

I took off my jumper and stood at the window in my nightdress. I rubbed my eyes, exhausted but not ready to sleep. A wheel of gulls cried ahead, and the window groaned. I felt the wind edging between the wooden frame, making me shiver. I imagined that in Leah's house her hands continued moving, winding the wool around the tool, thinning it, uncoiling it into threads, which cut into her swollen joints. Her knuckles hard as stone. Meg watching her steadily, sadly. I imagined Edward drawing the island, willing each part of it into being. Drawing me, my hands, my lips. I closed my eyes to block out the images. I don't know how long I stayed there, but when I opened them the edge of the yard was illuminated in pale light, and my insides were numb with cold.

December

One dawn, at the start of December, men came to the
beach to hack the whale's body up. Joan was with them,
gesticulating, shaking hands, laughing.

I watched from afar, on one of the hillsides.

The men worked methodically on the beach below.
One, who seemed to be the leader, held a clipboard. Their
boat had pulled a large cargo vessel behind it, where the
blubber and skin was being thrown.

From half a mile away, I could hear the axes swinging
and the belches as they cut into the whale's body. A smell
of meat and sweat descended, and by morning was faint.

The following night Reverend Jones told us the story of
what happened. He had brought whiskey for Tad and Tad
invited him in. I sat near the doorframe, hoping to catch
some news of Joan or Edward. Elis was bothering me, licking my hands. I held him still against my shins.

The men were with the National Salvage Council. Joan
had invited them to the chapel. They had carried all of the
parts of the whale away in large buckets. The Reverend
had offered them tea, and bread, and they had taken it on
the beach; one cup was still missing. They were all clever

folk, he said, though they refused to tell him their names. They said the whale would be very useful: the oil and blubber for fuel, the organs and skin for dog food and fertiliser. You make it sound like war is just around the corner, the Reverend had said.

Reverend Jones had asked if they needed help carrying the skeleton. He thought the fishermen could place a bone each on their vessels and meet the Council's boat further out at sea. They laughed, he said. One man mimed doffing his hat. They said, keep the bones.

A ship arrived in the night. No one saw it. Lukasz told us about it later. A ship full of children heading to Ireland, a planned stop-off for them to get bread and some water. After that when I looked out in the dark mornings I thought I could see their eyes glowing like a fox's, but it was just the dawn light on the rocks. Llinos found a paper label on the beach a few days later, for somebody named RUTH STERN. Ruth Stern was going to Ireland, and was three years old. If you asked Lukasz what the children were like, he only shrugged and said, they looked scared.

Morning, paper nailed to the door of every house. Tomos with a satchel of the papers and a hammer, and a pocketful of chocolate. The first page was a typewritten letter with an official-looking sign in one corner. It instructed us to fill our details into a grid on another page. A National Register, the order said, of every civilian, in the event of war. That Dr Joan Cable had been tasked with distributing and collecting them when complete.

Name, age, address, occupation, health conditions.

Tad studied the paper for a long time. What's this word, Manod, he said, turning to me, his finger poised beneath 'co-ordinating'. It means working together, bringing things together, I told him.

I had to fill in the details for each of us. I thought about lying and saying Tad was blind in one eye, or had a bad lung. That Llinos was younger than she was. I was distracted. The future seemed to gallop towards me. I wondered why Tomos had been tasked with nailing the letters, and not me. Against my own 'Occupation', I left the space blank.

SJCEG Disc 22.

Well, dear friends
Here we come
To ask your leave
To sing.

If we may not sing,
Then tell us in song
The way we should leave
Tonight.

> By wind or by sea
> Make your own way,
> We won't give you welcome
> Tonight.

*Collected 07.12.38 from G. Llan (b. 1898) and M. Llan (b. 1920),
residing Y Bwthyn Rhosyn (Rose Cottage). Call-and-response
folk song, with variation recorded in the south of the country,
Glamorganshire.*

Outside the chapel, a group of women and men stood around Joan, in a small circle. She was handing out pamphlets, laughing brightly. Llinos stood close to me, rather than joining her friends. She made small circles in the dirt with her shoe, and fiddled with the lace collar around her neck. The winter light was clean and cold, the sun falling in pale columns.

A group of men were examining a ram, a bulldog-nosed thing with a black face. Their dark suits were getting covered in dry grass from the animal's fleece, and each of them picked the pieces off and dropped them to the ground. Dai peered into the sheep's mouth, to look at its teeth. The ram's eyes rolled wild. When he let the jaw go, he patted the animal on the head, smoothed the curls between its eyes.

'How do I look?' Leah said, smoothing the skirt of her green dress down. I had found another needle, and finished it.

I almost laughed, the sight of the velvet against her boots trailing clumps of farm dirt.

'This is my best dress,' she said.

'You look lovely, Leah.'

'I have a dress for you,' she said, 'for Mari Lwyd. I've left it on your step.'

I thanked her. Llinos knocked into my hip, and I placed my hand on her cheek.

'What age d'you give him?' I heard one of the men ask about the ram.

The ram reared its head back, and the men clamoured to calm it, placing their hands together on its rump. They mumbled problems with their sheep like proverbs: blackleg, redwater, footrot, fly-strike pole worm.

~

In chapel, we sang psalms. Reverend Jones led the verses and we followed together, our voices swelling over the words. The chapel smelled of damp and we all shivered. I saw a leaflet in my father's pocket and pulled it out by the corner.

"UP BRITAIN!" it read. I placed it back into his pocket. He felt the movement and turned toward me. I smiled without showing my teeth. For the first time, I saw the way his hair parted at the crown on his head, leaving a tender, pink patch of skin.

The singing carried on around me. Our voices rose and fell together like the starling flocks that appeared sometimes in spring, and disappeared as quickly as they came. When I looked over to the front pew, Edward was recording the singing. I wanted to kick the machine over and snap the disc in two. I thought I saw from the corner of my eye Joan staring at me, but it could have been a trick of the light.

~

Outside the chapel, I walked to where my father was standing with the other fishermen. They were smoking, and one removed his hat when he saw me, and turned it in circles in his hands. He had a corsage in his jacket button, sea-thrift, a lonely lilac flower, half-dead.

Edward was speaking to other islanders. He spoke to Olwen for a long time, and then to her younger sister. Olwen looked well, though her dress gaped around her middle. She wore one in navy blue, with a patterned jumper over the top. Her sister wore one in dark yellow, with brown flowers. Her face was pink and her hair shone like a penny. The sister laughed, and touched Edward's arm.

'Oh!' I heard Edward say. 'Well, I do like your dress!'

'Aren't you cold, Manod?' Tad said, breaking me from my thoughts.

I shook my head. He wrapped his coat around me anyway, and kept his hand on my shoulder.

Preparations for Mari Lwyd had begun at the end of November. Geese and chickens had been slaughtered and frozen in the bwthyns. In one of the sheds behind the chapel, three horse skulls were removed from the chest they were kept in throughout the year. A group of men dusted their cobwebs and the small insects that covered them.

There were three horse skulls, of different sizes. Tad remembered when the third horse died, but no one on the island could remember the other two. The third horse belonged to a farmer who died when Tad was my age. His wife wore black, red and white every day with a tall traditional hat, Tad said. Tad said the horse died of a broken heart after his master, but there are other rumours. I had heard that the horse was killed by the farmer's eldest son so that it would not be taken for the Great War.

The horse skulls were carried down to the beach to be washed in the sea. The wives and children of the men who collected them decorated them, sewing yards of brightly coloured fabric to be hung from the back, like a mane, and painting small bells to go in the eye sockets. Sometimes, if a bell could not be found, they used eggs instead.

I didn't know who had decided to take the whale's skull from the beach. It appeared behind the chapel one day, near the shed where the horses' skulls were kept, as if the whale had emerged from the ground's surface, its bottom half still swimming.

My room was bathed in strange light when I woke. I went to the window and saw everything covered in a thin, silver layer of frost. Winter always came gradually, then suddenly. Our sheets and clothes had turned cold and damp, like they belonged to snails.

I found the dress Leah had been talking about at chapel, and pulled it over my nightdress. It was raspberry-coloured velvet, and I had to contort myself to zip it up at the back. I caught sight of myself reflected in the window pane, hunched over, merging with the grass. When I fastened the zip and began to pull, the nightdress became caught, and I tugged at it until I heard it rip. I removed the rest of the dress carefully and laid it over a chair. There was a mysterious brown stain on it, the size of a fist.

~

I heard a knock at the window. Edward was standing in front of the house, smartly dressed in a grey tweed suit. His glasses shone amber in the light. It shocked me, and I placed my arms over my nightdress to hide my breasts. I motioned for him to come round to the front door, but he shook his head.

I tried to open the window but couldn't. The cold must have jammed the wood shut against the frame. I pulled at the hinges for a while, trying to loosen them, until I saw Edward watching me on the other side and felt embarrassed.

'Could I ask you to translate one last word for me? Before I go?' he asked through the glass. His voice sounded strange, stilted.

He held up a piece of paper to the glass, writing in its centre.

'It means cockle,' I told him. 'Specifically a spring cockle, a young one. Younger than two years old. Some people leave them behind when they go gathering, so they can breed more the following year.'

I shivered.

'Right,' Edward said.

'What did you mean, before you go?'

'Didn't Joan tell you? We want to be home for Christmas. Two days from now.'

'Would you not stay for Mari Lwyd?'

'We'll see it in one of the mainland villages. There's a parade near Abergele.'

He put his hand absentmindedly up on the glass, fingers splayed. I copied him, and he took his hand away.

'I'll send you a copy of the book,' Edward said.

'I thought I was coming with you,' I replied.

'What?' Edward curled his hand around his ear. His ear was scarlet in the cold outside.

There were bees on the windowsill, some shrivelled and dry, others crawling along the crack between the window and its frame, drowsy with cold. A grey moth hovered half-way up the pane, knocking against the glass with a quiet sound.

I felt as though a stone had dropped in my stomach. I moved my tongue fatly around my mouth, probing the sharp edges of my teeth.

'I thought I was coming with you,' I repeated.

Edward laughed awkwardly. His breath misted up the glass in a near-perfect circle.

'You can come whenever you like,' he said.

'I mean with you, when you and Joan leave.'

'There's nothing stopping you.'

'So I can come with you?'

He put his hands roughly into the pockets of his jacket. His eyes darted around my face, never landing.

'I think the boat is fairly small on our crossing. We have all of our equipment, our papers. It might be better — I mean, more comfortable for you, if . . .'

He turned away, as though he heard someone approaching. He was blushing, with cold or embarrassment. I wondered if I was dreaming. My throat burned. He sighed.

'Manod. If I have led you to believe—Sometimes I get . . . carried away. I don't mean to—'

I walked quickly to the door and pulled it open roughly, but when I stood outside my fury turned to something else, dampened. What good would I do, making a scene? Joan would think I was savage. They might even put it in the book. I could hear Elis barking behind the house, and smell peat fires. I could hear the sea churning, the currents rising and falling.

'Do you remember the photograph Joan took of you?' Edward said, walking towards me. He looked as though he might take my hands in his, but he left them hanging limply at his sides. I thought how dirty his tweed jacket now looked, after his months on the island.

'I thought you might like to know we want to include it in the book, with your name. A thank you for your work with us.'

I imagined my picture in the book: my white dress and paper curls, like a doll. Next to the photograph of John, submerged in the sea, half-drowning and clutching for fish. I felt Edward watching me, waiting for my response. I looked back at the window, the interior warped by the thick glass. A pale square on the wall where a frame had been.

'Where are my embroideries?'

'Your embroideries?'

'Where are they? Can I have them back?'

'Oh. Yes, Joan has them. She must have forgotten to return them.'

I could hear Dafydd herding the goats towards their shelter, their cries as they crowded down the hill.

'She'll bring them for you when we leave,' he said. 'I'm sure she meant to tell you.'

I opened my mouth to speak, but Edward was already walking, quickly, out of the yard and to the path.

'We're leaving at eight,' he shouted over his shoulder. 'It's meant to be a good day.'

He said something else, swallowed up by the wind.

I went back inside and let the door close behind me.

I went straight to the harbour in the morning, long before the time Edward said they would be leaving. I had waited by the fire for Joan to bring the embroideries back. I pricked the back of my hand with a needle to keep myself awake. I wanted to see her. She never came.

It was a cold morning and I walked quickly. The sky darkened at the edges. I was wearing my chapel shoes, which were too big for me, hard leather that gleamed even in the low light.

I expected a crowd on the beach to watch the English couple leave, but it was empty. Further along the shore, Tad was loading his boat with the other fishermen to sell the last catches of the season on the mainland. The rowing boats looked the same: dark wood with pale metalwork, tied to one another with rope.

Reverend Jones was standing at the water's edge, fiddling lazily with his black-covered Bible. I walked quickly to him, shielding my eyes against the sand picked up by the wind. I called to him. Had he seen Edward and Joan? He looked surprised to see me.

'Are they taking a later boat?' I asked breathlessly. 'Where is everyone?'

'Later?' he said. 'They left just before dawn. In case the weather turned.'

He gestured across the water. It looked calm to me. The other fishermen were calling to him. He coughed, and turned to walk towards them. I followed. My hands were trembling, so I shoved them into the pockets of my coat.

'Did they leave anything for me?' My voice sounded far away.

'They didn't tell me if they did.'

'They had some of my embroideries. Joan was supposed to bring them back.'

He stopped, thinking, fiddling with the cuff of his jacket. I saw part of it was frayed.

'There are some papers in their room still. Something might be there.'

I looked for pity in his face, but found nothing. He walked on, then stopped suddenly and turned.

'They have a picture of you,' he said. 'I saw you in the darkroom.'

The picture from the first day. The silvery paper pegged onto that piece of string, my face slowly appearing.

~

I stood at the edge of the beach, where the wind blew my hair across my mouth and hid my face. The winter was with us now, and most of the men wore two jackets and rubber boots. When they weren't groping around with knots they blew into their hands, and rubbed them together. The men passed the boxes and buckets of fish to one another, loading up the boats. From far away they looked as though they moved together as one body, each of them in the same dark clothes.

Tad climbed into his boat with Dai, and Dai ducked up and down, emptying water from the boat's hull with a large bucket. Dai's boy Jacob sat in a boat on the shore, watching his father work.

Tad noticed me, and waved. His hat blew off into the water, and floated there like the head of a seal. The boats left the harbour slowly, and behind them the waves churned white, like a veil of lace stretching out towards my feet.

Their room was dark, the curtains drawn. A single shaft of light fell through the crack between them and illuminated the dust particles floating around me. There were two single beds covered with woollen blankets in a dark tartan pattern. The room smelled like every room on the island: straw, damp, animal.

I started with the bureau by the window, looking in every drawer. I searched the wardrobes, the chest, the small cabinet between the beds. I checked again, pulling the drawers out completely, tipping them upside down. The wardrobe doors swung open, empty. Under the beds was only a pile of the Reverend's books, a dark crucifix removed from the wall. Panic began to settle in my fingers. I looked again, leaving the drawers scattered, the bedclothes upturned. I was panting. The papers Reverend Jones mentioned were

on the bedside cabinet. As I lifted them, a thread of familiar red yarn fell to the ground, frayed at one end. My ears
were ringing. I knew that my embroideries were gone.

I let myself sit on the floor, my back resting against the
mattress. I twisted the red yarn between my fingers, trying
to calm my breathing. The papers caught my eye. They
were covered in rough notes and small drawings. I flicked
through them: drawings of gravestones, of hills, even of
the white eel from the western cave. I saw my name, and
it looked made-up. Manod Llan. 30/01/20. I saw the faces
of fishermen, their beards, hats, faces. Figures of children
running, women stooping to collect cockles and mend nets.
Sheep smudged into directions to the fish market.

I saw a curlew drawn on one page, stepping across the
blank water of a shallow tide-pool. The words 'storm' and
'death' written in Joan's neat hand. As I flicked through, I
realised there were no photographs, which meant they had
taken the one Joan took of me on the first day. I turned
the page again to find a sheet of longer notes. Edward's
handwriting.

*Close contact with nature brings a happiness few city dwellers
know – along with a lack of interest in material possessions.*

*I spend the night with the family of my assistant. The
father is a shore fisherman, a man of 40 years and 5 feet.
Two daughters, one being my assistant and the other a young
child. The older daughter is said to be 18 years old, unmarried,*

mature if inexperienced. Likely to be married off to a local man. The child is potbellied from her diet of bread and fish; her teeth chipped to points. There is no mention of a mother.

Below it, smudged ink, the echo of a whale's tail.

For the first time in a long time, I thought about when they found our mother. Lukasz had come from the lighthouse one evening and knocked on the door. I invited him in. I tried to stand in front of the unwashed pots and plates, the uneaten food that sat on them all. He would not look at Tad. He handed us the telegram and left.

Our mother had been found on a beach along the mainland coast, around twenty miles away, nestled between rock pools. She was found by two wealthy women, who were searching for fossils.

We went to see her the following week. I remember the journey being smooth, between tides. Llinos fiddled with something in her pocket and when I saw the white of them, realised what they were, I took them from her pocket and threw them into the water. She hung over the side watching them sink.

Llinos stayed outside, in a secretary's office. The secretary showed her a painting on the wall, white horses in a field at night, and gave her small toffees wrapped in foil.

Tad and I went down to the morgue, where Mam was brought out to us on a silver table. A man in a white coat pulled the sheet away. I held her hand, and it was cold. I saw a tiny thread trailing from her mouth. She was not my mother, but a dream of my mother. The skin of her arm was silver, half-fish, and her legs appeared as one fused stump.

I remembered the sailor who jumped from the boat in the card game. I wondered if that was how my mother felt.

Llinos stopped sleeping. She had pains in her belly, and when she got up from bed her nightgown was dark with blood.

'Am I ill?' she asked me, her eyes shining.

'No,' I replied.

I led her to the kitchen, and brought the tin bath in from outside. I brought water, cold, not wanting to light a fire and wake Tad up. I showed her how to clean herself up, and balled up her nightdress in a bucket of cold water. It was night and even Elis was sleeping. It felt like our secret. She leant on me as she crouched in the pan and splashed herself, her hand warm on my skin.

In bed I positioned myself behind her, wrapping my hands around her hips. I thought the warmth and pressure of my hands might help the aches. The moon was full and cast light on the wall. She made a bird with her fingers, and splayed her hand out, showing up a shadow on the other side of the room.

'Will you bring me back something from England?' she asked quietly, shifting her head to a new position on the pillow.

I hadn't thought about the fact that I'd have to tell her I wasn't going, that Edward and Joan had gone.

'Of course,' I lied.

Llinos sighed.

'I'll do my English exercises. Then I can visit you.'

She wriggled her hands under mine, and held on to my fingers. Her grip was tight, and twisted my fingers uncomfortably, but I didn't move. When I woke up, Llinos's back was soaked with sweat, her short hair curled into the nape of her neck in a perfect loop.

For Mari Lwyd, I chose two of Tad's lobsters to cook.

I turned them over and checked for eggs. They were cold from being outside, slow-moving. I placed the knife between the eyes, the way Tad had showed me, and pressed it down quickly.

I opened the body first, shucked each one down to their glowing insides, their green livers. The smell of them was familiar, and lingered on my hands.

I melted butter, added herbs. I gave the guts to Elis.

On the plate, the bodies curved together. I called Llinos down to eat. She said they looked like two faces looking at each other. The windows were white with steam, and Llinos traced our names on the glass in a neat row. The first time I had seen her write freely.

I remember a dress my mother wore, yellow with small white flowers. I remember her holding baby Llinos in the yard, singing to us. I must have been sitting on the step. When she turned, the material fanned to a perfect circle.

On the day of Mari Lwyd, the sky was tinged pink and the air damp and unseasonably warm, like the inside of a mouth. When the sun set I changed into my dress, and helped Llinos into hers. I moved her arms into the sleeves and saw how much taller she was, almost as tall as me. Her forehead was dotted with three red spots, and I ran my finger over them. I sat her in a chair in front of me and combed through her hair, easing out each wild knot. Llinos's hair would never be smooth but I separated it enough to plait it tightly on each side, tying the ends with green ribbon. Her dress was black, and the material had white ripples from some kind of dampness getting in.

We waited for the Mari Lwyd to reach us, when it was dark. The house creaked and we could hear the sea rumbling in the distance. Llinos saw the procession first, of men carrying the horses' skulls on long poles with trailing manes, the orange light of their candles coming up the hill.

'Tad is with them,' Llinos said, excitedly. 'He's leading them!'

There was something behind them I strained to make out.

They knocked on the door three times.

~

It was tradition to hand over food when the wassailing party reached you. Sometimes they came inside and ate with us. I told Llinos to get the bread and ale I had kept for the Mari. She shrieked with laughter at the sight of Tad's shoulders and pale beard underneath the horse's skull, and its golden brocade mane. I recognised the material from Leah's curtains.

'Thank you, young lady,' Tad-horse said, bobbing the horse's head up and down.

The food was passed along the men and women in the procession to a wheelbarrow at the back, pushed by a bored-looking Tomos. The other two horse skulls came to the door and Llinos stroked their bare noses. I couldn't work out who was underneath them. They told us riddles, as it was tradition to do, and we tried to answer them. Llinos whispered in the skulls' ears and kissed them on the cheek, and they gave her a cube of sugar.

I was watching when Tad gripped my arm. He lifted the skull from his head.

'We have a surprise,' he said.

I saw Tad's face before I saw the end of the procession.

His face was lit up. It looked young, and I glimpsed what he looked like as a child.

The whale's skull was carried by six men on their shoulders. Some of the older women on the island say that on Mari Lwyd the dead return for a night. The horses bring them – Rhiannon on her grey mare. The skulls tell you riddles and you outfox death and cheat it if you tell a riddle it can't solve. I whispered something into the whale's ear, so the men on either side couldn't hear it. Something my mother always used to say. The whale skull nodded twice and then shook its head. The people around me erupted in cheers.

I remembered my mother's face suddenly, like a flash of light on water.

I didn't sleep. I watched the light in the room change, heard the sounds of the Mari Lwyd party die down. I let my hands sew something without a plan. In my lap appeared a cormorant, turning its blue eye towards me, a pink ribbon around its neck. Tiny autumn leaves. A border of mussel shells. At dawn I heard the goats cry aimlessly, and put on my coat.

Ascending to the cliffs I watched the sun appear like snow on the water. I passed a fencepost holding the old skull of a sheep, yellow with age and exposure. A green caterpillar moved along the bridge of its nose. The caterpillar's front half reared up and waved from side to side. I remembered when Llinos was little, and believed she could communicate with insects. The caterpillar lost its footing and dropped to the ground.

A trail of smoke crossed from the mainland to the centre of the sky. From above, I saw something dark breaching the water's surface, a body flickering in and out of view. I looked across the water and something there understood what I wanted. I resolved to write a letter in response to Rosslyn's.

I'm going to the mainland. Taking Llinos if she'll come. I'll find work, buy a house.
   And God have Mercy, never marry.

I closed my eyes, the sea behind my eyelids turned the most brilliant red. When I looked again, the body was gone. The water bathing in its own light.

A Note on the Text

The island setting is fictional, but based on an amalgam-
ation of islands around the British Isles. While some island
communities continue to thrive, many of these places have,
over the last two centuries, seen declining populations,
increasingly harsh weather, the sale of land to private
owners, and younger generations moving to the mainland.
Particular influences on the novel are:

Bardsey Island (Welsh: Ynys Enlli), located off the Llŷn
Peninsula in the Welsh county of Gwynedd. In 1931, it had
a population of around 60 people. As of 2019, there is a
long-term population of 11, of whom 4 remain over winter.

St Kilda (Scottish Gaelic: Hiort), an isolated archipelago
in the Outer Hebrides of Scotland. The last population of
Kilda, numbering 36 people, was evacuated in 1930. All the
cattle and sheep were taken off the island two days before
the evacuation by the tourist ship *Dunara Castle*, to be sold
on the mainland. The island's working dogs were drowned
in the bay.

The Blasket Islands (Irish Gaelic: Na Blascaodaí), a
group of islands off the west coast of Ireland, forming

part of County Kerry. The islands were evacuated in 1953 due to population decline and increasingly extreme winter weather.

The Aran Islands (Irish Gaelic: Oileáin Árann), or The Arans (na hÁrainneacha), a group of three islands in Galway Bay, off the west coast of Ireland. In 1931, Robert J. Flaherty arrived on the islands to begin shooting his documentary about the Aran Islands, *Man of Aran*. The film later became notorious for its factual errors and fabricated scenes, including asking the islanders – who could not swim – to perform invented traditions in the sea, and creating an artificial family at the centre of the narrative, who were chosen from among the islanders for their photogenic qualities. As of 2022, 1,347 people call the Aran Islands their home.

Acknowledgements

It has been one of the greatest fortunes of my life to find the brilliant people who have brought this book into being. Thank you to my agent, Matthew Marland, for his belief in me from the start. Thank you to Sam, Tristan, and all at RCW for their faith and support.

Working with Mary Mount at Picador has been a dream. Thank you Mary, thank you Orla. Thank you to my extraordinary editor across the pond, Lisa Lucas, and her assistant Amara. Thank you also to the wonderful international publishers who have picked up my strange little book about Welsh fishermen, and taken it to new shores.

I'm indebted to writers who wrote accounts of their lives on the Blasket Islands, Bardsey Island, the Aran Islands and St. Kilda. These accounts of island life and community in the nineteenth and twentieth centuries inspired a number of events and details of daily life in this novel. Thank you to Brenda Chamberlain, Christine Evans, Andrew McNellie, Gearoid Cheaist O Cathain, Tomás Ó Criomhthain, Peig Sayers, Muiris Ó'Súilleabháin, and Donald John Gillies.

My wonderful family give me the support and motivation to keep writing. Thank you to my aunts and my late grandmother, for their unwavering support. A special thank you to the members of my Welsh and Irish family who will not get to read this book, inspired as it is by their lives. I thought of you always; your legacy of working and living with the sea, your journeys inland.

Thank you to my friends, for their encouragement and love over the years – Beth, Henry, Ella, Lucy, Sophia, Madi and Kat. I promise none of the terrible characters in this book are based on you.

Thank you to my colleagues at the University of Birmingham, for their support and enthusiasm for *Whale Fall*.

Thank you to my dad, who believes that all birds are holy.

Thank you to my mum, for everything. And thank you to George, my favourite reader.